The Shadow Wolf
BONNIE VANAK

MILLS
BOON®

First published in Great Britain 2012
by Mills & Boon,
an imprint of Harlequin (UK) Limited,   3 1 JUL 2012
Large Print edition 2012
Harlequin (UK) Limited, Eton House,
18-24 Paradise Road, Richmond, Surrey TW9 1SR

© Bonnie Vanak 2011

ISBN: 978 0 263 23037 6   117902340

ML4

Printed and bound in Great Britain
by CPI Antony Rowe, Chippenham, Wiltshire

Dear Reader,

Out of all the Draicon werewolves in my previous Nocturnes, Gabriel Robichaux is the most misunderstood and the most dangerous. A fierce warrior with a dark past, Gabriel has a secret to hide and will do anything to protect it.

But Megan Moraine threatens to topple every safeguard Gabriel has erected. Megan is a Shadow Wolf, Draicon who are outcast because they can turn invisible. She and her cousins escaped their island prison and are on the run from authorities. To protect the girls, Megan must team with Gabriel, the very Draicon she fears the most.

Trust doesn't come easily to either Gabriel or Megan. But they must learn to depend on each other to survive....

Happy reading!

Bonnie Vanak

In memory of my dear cousin, Margi Musarra. You loved your family more than anything else and always put their needs above your own. You will live on in our hearts and our memories.

Chapter 1

Please, don't throw us to the wolves.

Icy air blasted Megan Moraine as she pulled open Casa del Sol's etched glass door. The hotel's sprawling lobby gleamed with polished wood and mirrored columns. Beneath the cracked soles of her secondhand tennis shoes, the marble floor sparkled.

Motioning the twins to remain outside in the sticky Florida heat, she scanned for threats. The restaurant here was a safe house, but so was the oceanfront Naples, Florida, mansion they'd visited last night. When Megan had exposed the silver crescent moon birthmark, the homeowner's expression had turned ice cold.

"I don't like Shadows, but I'm generous. I'll

give you sixty seconds to leave before I call an Enforcer or send my mate after you," the Draicon werewolf had warned.

Sixty seconds didn't allow enough time to reach the car's hiding spot. Chased by a brutish male waving a meat cleaver, she and the girls raced down the beach. Megan spent the night guarding the twins, two seven-year-old girls who should have been tucked into soft beds instead of curling up on wet sand. As dawn streaked the gray skies, they'd snuck back to fetch the car.

More hostile Draicon could be inside, but she had no choice. Her jeans pocket held a few crumpled dollars. The aging Ford she'd hot-wired was running on fumes. She needed help to reach New Orleans and Alexandre Robichaux. The kindly Draicon secretly gave escaped Shadow Wolves new identities. He wasn't a soulless creature like his legendary Enforcer brother, Gabriel, who liked to make his captives bleed.

The girls' blue eyes widened as they scurried past the hotel lobby into the arched hallway. Megan felt more conspicuous when she saw the restaurant's linen-draped tables and polished silverware. The trick to blending was all in the act. Act like you belong, and people treated you that way. In a voice as impervious as a Palm Beach matron, she asked for seating on the terrace.

Their granite-topped table was half-hidden by a terra cotta planter. The terrace overlooked a lush garden of palms, ferns and tropical flowers. Best, she had a good view of the hotel entrance to eye new arrivals.

A smiling waitress in black trousers and starched white shirt sailed over, pen and pad in hand. Her gaze fell to Megan's right hand.

Damn. Megan clapped her left hand over the birthmark she'd forgotten to cover with cosmetics. She couldn't risk exposing her identity until they knew this was a safe house. But the waitress only smiled.

Megan glanced down at the heavy leather menu and cringed at the dollar signs. "One small glass of milk for them, and water for me, please."

"Cousin Megan, can't we have sausage and eggs?" Jenny pleaded.

"We can share," piped in Jillian.

"Maybe later."

The girls stared at the tabletop. Her heart broke at their crestfallen expressions. *I'm doing the best I can. I'm sorry I can't do better.*

The waitress hesitated. Megan lifted her chin. "That's all, thanks."

A lump clogged her throat as she studied her young cousins. Hair dye had turned their soft white-blond curls coarse and dull. Their shoulders were thin, their blue eyes glazed with sleeplessness. The matching strawberry shorts and flowered shirts she'd bought at a thrift shop were faded and ragged. Ever since they'd escaped the island prison, they'd been too quiet, forced to act far too old.

Soon. Sausage and eggs and heaps of whatever you want to eat. If we can just make it until our escort shows up.

Searching for hostiles, Megan scanned her surroundings. Only one customer had looked up at their arrival. The silver-haired man seemed more absorbed in his newspaper. Resentment and old hurt surfaced as she scented Draicon werewolves. Clustered together at a large table, they laughed as they dug into a big plate of sausage. They were her people, yet not.

Why do you hate us so much? We're not so different.

Not different, but feared, taunted and shunned by ordinary Draicon. Tired of being treated as inferior, Shadow Wolves had retreated to a small Caribbean island to raise their young. Six years ago, rogue Shadows—hoping to force their Draicon brethren into acknowledging them as equals—nearly exposed their race to humans. Worse, they sold their story to a popular American talk show. The program was stopped before it aired and a Draicon with the ability of mind control convinced network executives the story was fake.

Afterward, the influential Council of Draicon feared that all Shadow Wolves wished to embrace sedition and establish a new order. To contain Shadows, they raised a force field around the island. A steep bounty was placed on the heads of any escaped Shadow.

The waitress returned with a tray on her outstretched palms. She set down two large glasses of milk, a mug of steaming coffee, and three plates piled with sausage and eggs. Megan protested. The woman held up a hand.

"Someone canceled an order. Can't let good food go to waste. It's on the house." She winked.

The girls beamed and a chorus of thank-yous followed. Megan swallowed past a sudden lump in her throat at the woman's compassion.

"Thanks," she managed to say.

Caution returned as the waitress scribbled on her pad, then handed the check to Megan. "Enjoy. My name's Mitzi."

When the waitress walked off, Megan read the note. "You're among friends. Remain here and someone will be along to help you get out of shadow."

Even though the code phrase was correct, Megan hedged. There was a fat reward for capturing an escaped Shadow Wolf. Enforcers didn't care if the escapees were beaten and raped before being turned over.

Hot coffee burned her mouth as she took a deep swallow. Megan took a bite of the food. It was delicious, but she had no appetite.

The roar of a powerful motorcycle drew her

attention to the hotel entrance. A man parked the Harley, drew off a black helmet and swung a muscled leg over the saddle. Megan's heart raced. The rider's face was permanently stamped into memory from the photos circulated among Shadows of their worst enemies.

Black liquid sloshed as she slammed down her coffee cup. Her mouth opened and closed like a fish gasping for oxygen.

Gabriel Robichaux.

Oh God. She'd walked straight into a trap.

Megan looked around, desperate to escape, but it was too late. If they left now, surely he'd see them. She slid down her seat.

The power and raw charisma he exuded felt like a tornado as he ambled onto the terrace. Tight black leather pants hugged each inch of his rock hard thighs and taut buttocks. A Harley-Davidson T-shirt and steel-toed scuffed boots gave him a dangerous air. Stubble shadowing his angular jaw contrasted with his classical good looks, like a biker with the face of an angel. Dark brown hair curled down to his wide shoulders. His mouth was sultry and mobile.

Four women sitting at a nearby table gave him the twice-over.

If they only knew what exactly he was, they'd run away screaming. Draicon, like her. Only not like her. Not Shadow, outcast and shunned. He was an Enforcer, who returned escaped Shadow Wolves to their island prison.

No Shadow ever escaped the powerful Gabriel.

Megan glanced at the girls.

"Jenny, Jilly, remember how I told you Enforcers are the bad ones? How they hunt down our people and return them to the island prison?" When they nodded, she whispered to the girls. They nodded. Plan all set.

Megan sauntered toward the restroom. She had to pass him. Her palms went clammy as she felt him glance in her direction. Peripheral vision caught Mitzi nudging Gabriel.

Palms sweating, she raced into the women's room. Megan drew in a trembling breath. He could inconspicuously follow her in here, but at least she had a few moments.

Bracing her palms on the counter, she studied her reflection. The face in the mirror was strained and framed by dull black hair that hid her natural honey blond. Shadows edged eyes the color of deep lake water. The secondhand clothing was streaked with sand, but at least it wasn't the hated purple tunic Shadows were required to wear.

Megan summoned her magick. Unlike the twins, she was a Halfling and required energy to shift. Her body screamed, the starved cells needing nourishment from rare meat. Burning pain scraped across her raw flesh, but she focused. For the girls, she had to do this, had to become...

Shadow.

As if in slow motion, her hands and arms vanished. Megan squeezed her eyes shut. When she opened them, nothing showed in the spotless mirror.

She was invisible.

Until someone else came to use the restroom, she was stuck. A door opening by itself would raise suspicion.

By now the twins, shadows themselves, would be waiting by the car. Even though they were young, their powers were far more advanced.

Come on, come on, Megan silently implored. *Someone use the restroom.*

The door creaked open and she started forward, then stopped. Her knees felt like cooked spaghetti. Megan trembled wildly.

Hardened with ruthless intent, the face of a male Draicon poked inside. Gabriel.

He entered, looking beneath the stall doors. Stunned, she inched backward until hitting the wall. His nostrils flared as he straightened.

Oh dear heavens, he'd caught her scent.

Panic flared as he strode in her direction with smooth grace and stealth. Gabriel's dark brown eyes widened. They flashed amber, signaling the emergence of his wolf. Her gaze traveled from the chiseled jaw and hollowed cheeks, down to the T-shirt stretched tight over his broad chest, to his long, muscled legs.

Tight leather snugly cupped his bulging sex. Megan acknowledged her sudden flare of sexual interest. Sheer biology. He was the enemy, the one she feared most, but striking in his innate masculinity. The air sizzled between them, the chemistry so intense she couldn't ignore it.

Biting back a hiss, she bunched her fists.

"I know you're there, Megan," he said quietly. "You can't hide from me."

Impossible. She was invisible. But he advanced, boot heels clicking on the tile floor.

"Just come with me now, and don't make a fuss."

Like hell I will. Hugging the wall, she inched toward the door. Almost there, almost, she could make it, open the door and be gone….

Gabriel pounced. Steely arms encircled her waist. She twisted, snarled with all her might, but he had pinned her against his hard body.

Depleted of energy, she could not maintain shadow. But she'd be damned if she went down without a good fight.

Terror squeezed her heart as her body materialized. She writhed in his powerful grip, but he held tight. Then he freed one hand. Megan shrank back. *Here it comes.* He was going to hit her. That's what Enforcers always did. Just for laughs.

Instead she felt him caress her cheek. The gesture felt soothing and erotic. Gabriel bent his head and brushed aside her hair. He was inhaling her scent. Surprised, she stopped struggling. Enforcers didn't care about their captives. She'd heard they only punished and brutalized. Alarmed at the rising tide of desire, she wondered if Gabriel's methods were even crueler than other Enforcers. Lower her defenses and then strike like a snake.

A tantalizing scent of leather, pine and spicy male filled her senses with erotic awareness. The space between her legs felt open and wet, wanting. Well aware of the distraction, Megan resumed her struggles to get free. But she was too exhausted.

Warm breath feathered over her cheek as he bent his head. "Shhh," he murmured. "It's all right. Everything will be all right. Sleep now."

This was the true danger, his deep, hypnotic voice lulling her into doing as he wished. Megan felt her eyes closing.

He pushed a hand through her hair, the gesture almost tender. Just before she passed out, she felt a sensual brush of his mouth across her neck as if Gabriel marked her.

Then the grayness turned black, and everything else faded into shadow.

* * *

"Dammit."

This was not how he had envisioned starting his long-awaited vacation. Gabriel stared at the unconscious woman slumped in his arms. Asleep, without the spark igniting her sea-blue gaze, she looked defenseless and young. Long dark lashes feathered against her cheeks. He nuzzled the top of her head, detecting the faint odor of hair dye. She was small, but her slender body looked capable of a good, hard fight.

Lifting her carefully into his arms, he stepped into the hallway. "Mitzi," he addressed the woman racing toward him. "Tell Jay to pull the Expedition by the back. Did you get the twins?"

"They're in the kitchen." His employee looked upset. "They're terrified. They're just kids, Gabriel."

"I know." Aware of his arousal, he shifted Megan in his arms, wondering why she'd caused such an intense reaction.

"You're going to have to do a major mind sweep of all the customers. Some were pretty upset when the twins started crying. Jay and I told them the police were on their way."

Gabriel cursed again. This went all wrong. Then again, nothing ever went exactly right when he was called in to deal with a Shadow Wolf.

"Breakfast on the house for everyone." The restaurant could afford it. It had turned over a profit ever since he'd purchased it ten years ago.

Jay, the restaurant's manager, hurried over. "Want me to put her in the truck, too, Gabe?"

"No," Gabriel said, more sharply than he'd intended. "Take care of the customers until I can do a little mind cleansing."

He felt protective, even territorial, of the unconscious woman. She felt soft in his arms. Another uncomfortable surge of arousal raced through him. Breathing in deeply, he caught the unfamiliar, odd smell of something faintly sinister, as well.

This Shadow must have come into contact with evil forces.

Using the restaurant's private kitchen exit, Gabriel headed for the SUV and settled her in. He gently smoothed her hair, disturbed at the lines of strain on her face. A low hiss escaped him as he saw a purpling bruise on her forehead.

Gabriel growled softly, wanting to find whoever dared to hurt her so he could demonstrate the power of his fists.

"You're safe now," he told her.

He went into the kitchen. The twins were huddled together on a chair, their eyes wide, holding each other's hands. Sending waves of reassurance into their minds through his powers, Gabriel squatted down to their level. "All will be well, *mes petites.* I'm going to take good care of you."

Then he waved a hand, telepathically commanding them to sleep and instructed Jay to put them into the back of the SUV. Gabriel called his housekeeper.

"Jean, we're having company. I need you to go shopping for twin girls, age seven. They're about 50-55 pounds. Get a bunch of shorts, shirts, enough sizes in case they don't fit and charge it to my card."

He hung up, went into the restaurant and planted subtle suggestions in the minds of the customers, nothing but a heated squabble between an irate husband and his wife. Even the pack of Draicon werewolves acquiesced. Everyone smiled and nodded, except for the silver-haired man folding his paper and setting it aside.

The man gave Gabriel a small, knowing smirk. His blood went cold. He tried again, probing the man's mind—just a squabble, no one hurt, nothing to see....

It felt like he'd smacked against a concrete wall. Gabriel inwardly winced, resisted rubbing his temples from the small spike of pain.

Fine. Gabriel let loose all his powers and sent them barreling into the man, like spraying him with a shotgun blast. The silver-haired man rubbed his head and dropped his gaze.

Satisfied, he went into the kitchen and gave Jay instructions to deliver the Harley to his island home.

Gabriel slid behind the wheel of the Expedition, glanced at the terrace. The silver-haired man was eating his breakfast.

The sun beamed strong and bright on the shimmering pavement as he drove away. Air conditioning blew through the vents inside the vehicle. When his cell rang, he fished the phone from his pocket.

"Robichaux," he stated.

"Whoa, you sound serious."

Gabriel glanced in the rearview mirror at his cargo. "Something unexpected came up. Have to cancel."

Silence hung in the air. Then Raphael spoke again. "Just as well with me. The rest of us couldn't see all that time for male bonding when we'd be gone from our mates and Alex. Well, Alex is seeing someone. Finally."

Joy and dismay collided together. Gabriel's hand tightened on the steering wheel. "Who? She's not…a Shadow, is she?"

"No, she's regular Draicon."

It was about damn time his older brother had some happiness. Alex had been grieving for his mate and child for the past three years. Ever since…

My fault, Gabriel thought, feeling the familiar sting of guilt. *All my fault.*

No time for the luxury of grief. "I'll be on the island for a few days. Contact me on an emergency basis only," he said.

"Ah, got it." Raphael sighed. "I thought you were done with this, Gabe."

"I was, until I got a call from Jay. No one else in the area is available so I have to deal with this case. There are kids involved, two little girls."

His brother cursed softly. "Everything okay?" Raphael sounded worried.

"Nothing I can't handle." Gabriel thumbed off the phone.

His grin died as he glanced again at the rear-view mirror. Gabriel maneuvered the SUV into a grocery store parking lot. He pulled into a space, left the engine running. With its darkened windows, no one could see inside the Expedition.

He powered up the small laptop sitting on the dash. Gabriel typed commands and called up the necessary information on his new adult charge.

Megan Moraine. Single, age 26. Reported missing from the island five days ago, with twin sisters Jennifer and Jillian Sullivan, her cousins. Grandmother deceased one week from natural causes. Suspect last reported seen in Naples, Florida, and is Halfling, but extremely clever and dangerous. Twins are full-blooded

Shadow and considered lethal. Use of extreme force in apprehension is approved.

Lost in thought, he switched off the computer and glanced backward at the sleeping Megan. His chest felt hollow as he studied the twins. They were too thin, pale and looked totally defenseless.

"You're safe," he murmured. "Sleep now, *mes petites.*"

His gaze slid to Megan. If Megan Moraine discovered his secret, he was screwed. He'd just have to make certain she never did.

To her, he was the enemy. For their own safety, she and those precious little ones must keep believing that lie.

If anyone found out otherwise, they'd all be on the run. For their very lives.

Chapter 2

A monster stalked her dreams, a snarling beast on two legs with red eyes and fur dark as midnight. "Trust me, Megan," it grated out as blood dripped from its sharp fangs. "I won't hurt you." But she was terrified because she knew it would drag her back to the island prison and laugh as it raked its claws across her cold skin so she would die slowly in agony.

Megan awoke with a small cry. *Just a dream. It's just the same dream you've had for years. Snap out of it.*

Someone wanted her dead. The threat lingered in the air like wood smoke. A dark-haired, handsome stranger with eyes that flashed amber; a walking, talking epicenter of lethal grace.

Gabriel Robichaux.

Cringing, she took a deep breath, expecting to be tied to a cold steel table, a metal tray of sharp instruments nearby.

But the surface beneath her was soft. Megan lifted her legs. No restraints. She was lying on a bed facing a bank of windows overlooking the Gulf of Mexico. Fingers of crisp white clouds streaked the sharp blue sky.

No purple tunic and matching pants, either.

Delicious smells of frying bacon came from downstairs. It enticed and cajoled. Food, she needed food, her head ached from hunger, the hollow pit in her stomach demanded energy.

She looked around. The cheerful powder-blue-and-lilac bedroom had a white bamboo dresser, glass-topped table and two chairs with floral prints. Megan touched her head, trying to get her thoughts squared.

"You never ate your breakfast, so I fried eggs. I advise you not to skip another meal or you'll fade into nothing, and not just because you're a

Shadow Wolf," came a deep, laconic voice from the doorway.

Tensing, she sat up, fists ready to strike. Now she remembered. Gabriel had hypnotized her into sleeping. Panic squeezed her insides.

"Where are they?" she demanded.

He leaned against the doorjamb, thumbs hooked through the belt loops of faded jeans. Rolled up at the sleeves, a blue chambray work shirt displayed his strong, tanned forearms. His feet were bare. A black cowboy hat tilted over his brow. "On the table, getting cold." In his deep Louisiana drawl, "table" was pronounced "tay-bull."

She threw back the thick duvet, swung her legs over the bed's side. Her feet touched soft carpeting. For a moment, she wriggled her toes, basking in the luxury. Megan struggled to fight the dizziness. "My cousins. What did you do with them, you bastard?"

"They're fine."

"If you hurt them, I'll..." The threat was empty, and they both knew it.

"Is this part of your torture technique? Keep

us separated, make me think the worst? Why not just kill us and get it over with?"

A frown dented his forehead. "I don't torture Shadows," he said mildly.

"Cousin Megan!" Two miniature tornadoes flew into the room and bounded on the bed. They crashed against her.

Hiding a wince at her sore arms, she held them tight. "Are you okay?" She smoothed back their hair, studied their expressions.

"Gabriel made us bacon and eggs and sausage," Jenny said, glancing shyly at him.

"And toast with orange marmalade." Jilly burped. "'Cuse me."

Gabriel made a sound suspiciously like a chuckle, but looked indifferent. Masking her anxiety, Megan smiled at the girls. They wore identical pairs of bright pink shorts and pink scoop-necked shirts. On their feet were new cuffed socks and sneakers.

Megan touched a corner of Jenny's shirt. "Where did you get these?"

"Gabriel had his housekeeper buy these for us. No more purple uniforms," Jenny told her.

"Gabriel took us here to his island to keep us safe," Jilly told her.

Megan tightened her grip on her niece. How could she tell her that Gabriel had abducted them? In some ways, her young nieces were still innocent, despite the island's harsh living conditions. She didn't want to scare them.

Instead, she gave a reassuring smile and changed the subject. "Did you get outside and see the Gulf of Mexico?"

If the girls had explored the island, she could figure out how to access the mainland and formulate an escape plan.

"Gabriel took us to the beach and we found some seashells by the water, but he didn't want us to go far," Jenny piped up.

She hid her disappointment.

"I wanted to check on Megan. We can go out later, Jenny," Gabriel said.

Jenny beamed. Megan studied her enemy, shocked he had discerned the difference between the girls. Few could tell them apart.

She had to regain her strength. Somehow, there was a way off this island, and she would find it. Megan braced her hands on the bed.

Going to do this, must do this. She managed to stand, but her knees gave way. With an involuntary cry, she fell back onto the bed. Oh this was bad, so very bad.

Eyes wide with fright, the twins stared. "Cousin Megan?" Jilly's voice trembled.

Gabriel detached himself from the doorway. He flashed a winsome smile at the girls. "Jenny, Jillian, why don't you go into the playroom while I have a little chat with your cousin?"

Dread pooled in her chest as the girls scrambled away.

He gave her a critical once-over. "When did you last eat?"

Her stomach growled a protest. "I'm fine."

"You're weak and dangerously low on energy," he countered, his gaze sweeping over her. "Where were you hiding out?"

"Rio. You know, de Janeiro in Brazil. I had a hankering for a mojito," she shot back.

He rubbed his temple. "Tell me."

The command was soft, threaded with steel. She felt compelled to obey. "Couldn't get here right away, had to diffuse the trail. Spent three days in the Bahamas first...lived off fish, the girls did…I gave them my share, couldn't catch much, had to lie low. Hitched a ride with a fisherman headed to Florida."

"Then how did you use up all your energy?"

Gabriel was a mind manipulator, able to coax hidden thoughts from reluctant victims. Horrified at how easily she'd confessed, she mustered her strength and bolted for the door. He hooked her around the waist. "Easy," he muttered. "Relax, *chère,* I'm not going to hurt you. But I will have answers."

Megan sagged in his arms. Her trembling hands couldn't grasp the doorknob. Pain throbbed from the rail spike hammering into her skull. Oh, the hunger was bad now, so bad, the craving for protein screaming its need.

Gabriel helped her sit on the bed. He picked up the cordless phone on the nightstand and dialed. He gave a crisp order for bacon, sausage and eggs and hung up, giving Megan a thoughtful look.

"Food first, then a hot shower. I'll ask Mrs. Hemmings to find clothing that fits." His heated gaze swept over her again, making her shiver. "You're a size twelve, right?"

Outraged, she glared. "I'm a size eight."

A smile tugged the corners of his mouth. He'd tricked her. Again.

"How the hell did you let yourself get this bad?" he demanded. "Didn't you make plans, have supplies?"

Megan looked out the window.

"The truth, Megan. Why haven't you eaten?"

With all her might, she shuttered her thoughts. Instead of invading her mind, Gabriel ran a thumb across her palm. The electrical contact sizzled, creating a shiver of erotic awareness. Megan stared at his strong, tanned fingers. He turned over her hand, frowned at the reddened scratches on the back.

"You got jumped. Someone stole your money," he guessed.

"The fisherman smuggling us off Shadow Wolf island demanded more money than we'd planned." Megan yanked her hand away.

"You're a Shadow. Why didn't you just steal money when you got to the States?"

"I'm no thief."

"Then I suppose the car with your scent all over it is a rental?" he drawled.

Color ignited her cheeks. "I put an envelope filled with money and a note in the door of the owner's home. It's worth more than the price of the Ford, which has leaky oil gaskets, bald tires and finicky brakes. I might be a Shadow—" she spit out the word "—but we have integrity. Unlike you Normals, who turn in your own people for money. Because we are Draicon, like you. Like it or not, that's a fact."

"Normals?"

"Stop acting as if you have no idea what I'm talking about. Normals. What you ordinary Draicon call yourself, what you insist we call you. You think you're normal and we're not just because we can perform magick before puberty, unlike you, and we can shift and become invisible, unlike you."

She gave him a pointed look. "With our gifts, I'd say we're superior to Normals. Except I'm not racist. Unlike you."

Amber glowed in his eyes. His wolf was emerging. As he raised his hand, Megan braced herself for the slap. Instead, he dropped his hand to her forehead, ran a thumb over the bruise.

"Some of us are anything but normal," he muttered.

A brisk knock at the door announced the arrival of a cheerful, rounded woman bearing a wood tray. On the tray was a large china plate piled with food, silverware, a napkin and a tall glass of orange juice. Megan nearly moaned at the savory smells of bacon, sausage and fried eggs. The woman set down the tray on the nightstand, accepted Gabriel's thanks and left.

Megan picked up the fork. Plastic, she noticed ruefully. Not much use as a weapon. This Draicon wasn't a fool. She poked at the eggs.

"It's not poisoned."

His voice, close to her ear, made her jump. Megan speared a sausage, turned it over. "Sure, right."

"If I wanted to drug you, *chère,* I'd merely put you to sleep with a mind suggestion, like I did back at the restaurant." Amusement laced his tone. His gaze grew stern. "Now eat."

Her hands shook so much she could barely bring the fork to her mouth. Eggs spilled onto the tray. Embarrassed, she shuffled the food around the plate. Gabriel paced over to the window and stood before it. Megan quickly ate, then wiped her mouth with a paper napkin. She drank the orange juice, feeling the throbbing hunger ease.

"Thanks for the food," she managed to say.

Gabriel turned around. Shafts of yellow sunlight angled into the room, falling on him like a spotlight. Breath caught in her lungs. Denim jealously hugged every inch of his hard, muscled legs. He was gorgeous, with the face of a fallen angel, secrets lurking in those swamp-dark eyes. The sheer sexuality felt like a blast of heat in the air-conditioned room.

She wondered what it would feel like to run her hands over his firm muscles, splay her fingers on that hard chest, feeling his heart race with the same anticipation she felt.

He's a cold, soulless killer, she sternly reminded herself. Megan drew in a breath, inhaling a spicy, rich aroma, like expensive men's cologne. Instinct told her it was his own natural scent. Damn, he smelled good.

His knowing smile warned he knew she'd checked him out. Megan squashed her irritation.

"Can I take a shower alone, or are you playing guard dog outside the bathroom, too?"

"Through there is the main guest bath." He pointed at a closed door. "Need help getting undressed?"

"I can manage."

"I can wash your back," he offered in a deep, laconic drawl.

Shivers raced through her. Megan envisioned herself in the shower, Gabriel running the soap down her back, gently caressing her slippery skin with his big hands, cupping her hips, pulling her against his naked body….

Not in this lifetime. "I always watch my own back," she muttered.

"Watch or wash?" he asked softly.

"Both. Because I never know when someone's going to stick a knife in it."

His gaze grew thoughtful. "I'll get the clothing for you. There are fresh towels and everything else you need in the bathroom."

When she didn't move, Gabriel sighed. "Come on, I'll help you."

As he grabbed her upper arm, Megan flinched. His gaze narrowed as she went to her feet.

"Take off your shirt," he ordered.

A violent trembling seized her. This was it, then. After all she'd gone through, constantly moving to avoid the sexual threats, keeping herself pure because she had vowed never to give herself to a man unless it was done with love, it came down to this.

"Do you always molest your captives?" she bit out.

He was far stronger and bigger, but she'd go down kicking and screaming. And biting.

"I'm not going to hurt you," he said, more gently this time. "Take off your shirt."

Color flooded her cheeks. She struggled to lift the threadbare green polo shirt over her head. He helped.

In her faded bra, she hugged herself, feeling cold and exposed and vulnerable. But anger, not lust, glinted his dark eyes. His mouth compressed to a thin slash as he traced one of the purpling bruises on her arms.

"Who did this?"

"I fell down the stairs."

"Megan, who hit you?"

Rather than have him yank it from her mind,

she settled for the truth. "The fisherman on the boat that smuggled us to the Bahamas. Said he'd heard Shadow females were incredible in bed, and he planned to find out. He beat me and threatened to hit the girls unless I cooperated."

Gabriel's breath eased out in a violent hiss.

"I made a deal with him. Said sex was better when Shadows weren't in physical form. If he could catch me while I was in shadow, I was all his. He liked the chase."

"That's why you were low on energy. You were invisible the entire trip to the Bahamas."

"I escaped at a cost. I thought I could make up for it by catching fish when we landed at the Bahamas, but the fishing was lousy and the girls were hungry. In addition to trying to molest me, the fisherman fed us only scraps."

"You haven't eaten properly for five days. Damn," he muttered.

Suddenly she felt drained beyond words. "Is show and tell over with now? Can I get dressed?"

Gabriel didn't say anything. He continued tracing the ugly bruises on her arms. His touch was gentle and oddly soothing, as if he wanted to erase her pain.

"What's his name?" His gaze was hard, but his voice was as soft as his touch.

She saw no reason to protect the man, since he was taking advantage of helpless Shadows. "He calls himself Devin Andrews, but we know him as Grouper. He likes deep-sea fishing, and uses that as his cover. His boat name, too."

"Good." He jerked his hand away, as if touching her scorched him. Gabriel turned his back. "Take your shower, and after, I have liniment for those bruises to help them heal faster. You're still too weak for your body to effectively heal itself."

"Is this your modus operandi?"

A half smile touched his full mouth as he glanced at her over his shoulder. "My what?"

"Being solicitous toward your victims before you kill them and collect the bounty on their heads."

Gabriel's expression softened. "I won't hurt you, *chère.*"

Right. She wouldn't gamble on that.

"I do have a few rules. Just as I told the twins.

Any problems or concerns, you bring them directly to me. You can't escape this island, so forget trying. You will eat and you will maintain your energy. No one will hurt you here, you're perfectly safe. But you aren't leaving."

Feeling his gaze burn into her back, Megan opened the door and walked into the bathroom. She closed the door firmly and found a fluffy white robe hanging on a peg behind it. She carefully shrugged into it.

The bathroom was larger than her bedroom at home, and the opulence made her feel shabby in comparison. Lilac rugs scattered over gleaming white marble floors. Wrinkling her nose at the color, she sidestepped them. In the corner was a glass shower with a window overlooking the beach.

Curious, she pulled open a cabinet drawer. Inside was an assortment of child's bath toys, including a well-worn rubber duck. A reluctant smile touched her face as she took out the duck and closed the drawer. Gabriel's guests included children. Nieces and nephews?

What was it like to be indulged, spoiled and pampered by a male as powerful as Gabriel?

To have everything you wanted to eat, pretty dresses to wear and all the knowledge at the tip of your fingers instead of having to hide books and wear ugly dark grape clothing? Her smile faded as she dropped the duck by a stack of towels on the counter. She grabbed a washcloth and soap, stared in bemusement at the twin shower heads and the strange fixtures.

Torn between pride and longing, she set down the washcloth and soap and returned to the bedroom.

Gabriel sat on her bed, touching her pillow with a thoughtful look. His cowboy hat was on the nightstand. He glanced up.

"I don't, the shower, the faucets..." Her voiced trailed off and she felt very stupid.

A wide grin tugged his full mouth upward. "Oh yeah. I got confused the first time the plumber installed the new fixtures. Shoulda heard me yell when I got cold water instead of hot."

He sprang off the bed, all grace and smoothness. Inside the shower, he worked the faucets, careful to step out of the way as he demonstrated the spray.

Gabriel stepped outside the shower. Megan gave him the first real smile she'd felt in days.

"Thanks. I thought I might need an engineering degree just to take a shower."

He tipped back his head and gave a deep, throaty laugh. Her heart skipped at the delightful sound. Surely anyone who laughed like that couldn't be as evil as they said.

"I like how you laugh. You're not what I thought."

Startled, she realized she'd spoken aloud. Gabriel stopped laughing. Megan shivered again, but this time from a deeper, more intense need.

A predatory look crossed his face. When he grasped her shoulders in the gentlest touch, she felt drawn toward him. His gaze fell on her mouth. Amber flashed in his eyes as she moistened her lips and parted them. Megan took a step forward, captivated by the smoldering hunger in his gaze. Her body yearned, her hands reached out to touch him in turn. She could almost feel his lips against hers, warm, authoritative, demanding….

Just as quickly, he stepped back, dropped his

arms. "Go take that shower, and I'll find the clothing and liniment."

The door slammed behind him with a violence that shook the hinges.

After her shower, Megan used the liniment Gabriel had left, dressed in the clothing he'd put on the bed and began planning her escape.

She slipped down the hallway and paused before a large, masculine bedroom at the corridor's end. Drawn by the rich spicy scent that was Gabriel's, she walked inside.

The bed was large as a car, with a crimson duvet and a hand-carved mahogany headboard. She shivered, imagining his big body on it, sweat gleaming on his brow, dampening his dark hair, his long legs twisted in the sheets after a hot bout of lovemaking....

Stop it.

The windows boasted splendid beachfront views. Coconut palms, their green leaves swaying in a gathering breeze, framed shimmering sand and tranquil Gulf waters. French doors opened to a wraparound balcony. Megan went outside.

The mainland seemed close enough to swim for it. But what about the twins?

On the bayside, a fishing boat, a sleek yacht and a rowboat were moored to the dock. Powering the fishing boat or the yacht meant noise. However, if she had Jenny create a distraction, they could use the rowboat. She disliked asking her cousin to use powers she had been taught to curb, but it was necessary if they were to escape.

A few hundred yards from the dock was a single-lane causeway and a bridge connecting it to the mainland. Megan spotted an outboard boat near the bridge. The boater started the engine, heading in her direction. Sweat gathered on her brow as he passed the house.

A man with silver hair. It was too far away to be sure, but she'd swear it was the same man from the hotel restaurant.

What did he want? Why was he following them? Was he a rescuer? Or like Gabriel, another enemy who desired the healthy bounty on their heads?

Gabriel should know. Megan's pulse sped up. She couldn't risk telling him, the enemy she couldn't trust. What if he were working with the silver-haired man?

The only person she could trust was herself. The twins relied on her. She had to get them off the island.

Megan found the twins in a large, airy room, playing dolls before a wood dollhouse. Her heart twisted. She hated having them on the run again.

Better running than dead. Because that's what Gabriel would do. He might be all smooth Cajun cowboy charm on the outside, but he was nastier than the other Normals. Gabriel would soothe them into thinking all was well, and then…

Megan shuddered. She motioned to the girls, who reluctantly abandoned the toys.

"We're leaving soon. When we do, just stick close to me, okay?"

Jenny looked upset. "But I like it here. Gabriel's nice. He promised to make us a nice dinner and we can each have a doll of our own. He wouldn't hurt us. He's…"

Squatting down, she took her cousin's small,

trusting hand into hers. "Honey, we have to get you to New Orleans, remember?"

Jenny brightened. Both twins had asked Megan why they were headed to New Orleans until she told them about hoping to find a relative there. More information was needed before telling them the relative was their father. The girls must not have their hopes raised and crushed. They'd already endured too much on the island.

Megan dreamed of finding their father, a man who would smother them with love and protection and send them to school, instead of learning with smuggled books. In the city, she'd blend and find others like her. Together they'd work to free all Shadows from captivity so future generations wouldn't fear imprisonment again.

Megan went downstairs into the living room. Arched windows looked out onto the green Gulf of Mexico. White cypress walls gave the living room an airy feel that flowed onto the beach. The furniture was durable, but expensive.

Megan peered into the kitchen. The housekeeper was cleaning the counter, her car keys out on the table.

She ran upstairs to join the twins. When the housekeeper popped her head in the doorway and announced she was leaving, Megan felt a rush of relief.

"I just wanted to see if you needed anything," Mrs. Hemmings said.

"We're fine. Thank you for the lovely meal."

"That was Mr. Gabriel who did the cooking." The woman studied her so intently, Megan felt like an animal in a zoo.

"You take good care of yourself, honey. Things will be fine from now on. You're safe here. Mr. Gabriel, he's a good man. You can trust him."

The woman could not know the delicate intricacies of their world. Regret filled Megan. She wanted badly to trust someone. Too much was at stake to risk it.

When the housekeeper left, Megan retrieved their backpacks and returned to the girls.

They were leaving. Right now.

Chapter 3

Sprawled on a lounge chair on the rear deck, Gabriel studied the sky for signs of the approaching hurricane. Just an hour ago, the water mirrored a blue sky sharp as a sickle. Now puffy indigo clouds drifted on the horizon, and lacy whitecaps tossed their heads back and forth.

He had to get them off the island soon.

Picking up an icy water bottle, he took a deep swallow and thought of Megan's pink mouth, the way her teeth worked at her lower lip, her delicious floral fragrance. The natural sensuality of her throaty voice, the spark of passion in her eyes, her sweetly rounded hips swaying as she walked.

His body tightened as he remembered her rosy mouth parting as if anticipating his kiss. The sultry awareness in her eyes, the longing for connection. How sturdy and soft her shoulders felt beneath his caressing fingertips.

He'd almost kissed her. Megan Moraine aroused him in a way no escaped Shadow ever did. He had to keep his distance. Even if her mouth was so damn soft and wet.

The haunting loneliness dogging his steps tormented him with a bitter memory. Another woman, years ago, her eyes filled with love, then growing wide with horror....

Your eyes, Gabriel, oh your eyes!

Cussing, he set down the bottle and fished out his cell. Gabriel punched in the same number he'd called ten minutes earlier. The Friend he needed to escort Megan and the little girls to the next safe house still wasn't answering and his voice mailbox was full.

Deeply troubled, he thumbed off the phone. He hedged moving Megan and the twins until he felt certain they would be safe. Each Friend, a guide who would help an escaped Shadow Wolf to the next safe house, was known just to one link in the chain. Only Gabriel knew all of them. And the fact that he'd called all the others and got no answers from them, either, worried the hell out of him.

Someone had infiltrated their network. He had to stay deep undercover. If anyone discovered his secret...

Muscles on his back contracted, as if his skin anticipated the twenty lashes the Council of Draicon would order. Next they'd ensure his gene pool was permanently drained.

The back door banged. He'd trip-alarmed the property to prevent Megan from leaving and he'd sabotaged the boats. Nostrils flared, he picked out the scent and relaxed.

"Mr. Gabriel? I finished cleaning the downstairs and I'm headed out now."

"Thanks, Jean. I left an extra something in your envelope for all your hard work. Won't need you for a few days."

Flushing with pride, she shook her head. "You're too good to me, Mr. Gabriel. You'd better leave soon. Storm's coming in, will be here by tonight, they say."

"We'll be fine," he assured.

The middle-aged woman looked worried. "There's something about that woman, Miss Megan. She reminds me of the war refugees who came to my home country years ago. That one has been hurt, badly."

She has. A fierce protective need rose to keep Megan from ever being hurt again. Gabriel made a mental note to find the sonofabitch who had beat her, and let him know the raw power of his raging wolf. "Don't worry, they're in good hands."

He watched her head for her ancient Lincoln, heard the engine start with a smooth purr. Gabriel had personally fine-tuned it for her. When the car reached the main road and hit one of the lasers, a small alarm went off. Gabriel knew Jean was safely off the island.

Gabriel also knew Megan hid something important. Yet he hesitated using his magick on her. He admired her resolute courage and love for the twins. Yanking information from her mind felt like a violation of her stubborn spirit. What would it feel like to be so demonstrative, to give and receive love without fear? To have someone know your true self so intimately?

A hollow ache settled in his chest. Hell if he'd ever know. No one would ever get that close. They wouldn't like his dark side.

Suddenly the prickling sensation returned. Gabriel called his housekeeper, asked if she'd noticed anything odd as she'd left the island. She hadn't.

"I'm on the mainland and almost home. Do you need me to return?"

"No. Everything's fine. If you don't hear from me the next couple of weeks don't worry, Jean." He hung up. The feeling grew stronger.

Gabriel bolted to his feet. Wolf senses picked out a strange scent. Though faint, this was darker, the foul stench of something that enjoyed twisting the limbs off screaming victims. Not Morph. Morphs, former Draicon who killed a relative to gain greater power, couldn't access the island because of its protective magick shield.

Vaulting over the railing, he landed on the ground fifteen feet below. Sand kicked up beneath his heels as he ran. As he hooked a hard right, an explosion *ka-powed* on the bayside.

No longer could he hold back the beast.

Tipping back his head, he released a long, low howl.

One minute man, the next beast. Digging his paws into the soft sand, he ran toward the bay.

"Hit the ground!"

Water splashed over them as shrapnel flew through the air and landed in the bay. The twins fell on the boat dock and Megan threw herself over them, shielding their bodies with her outstretched arms. Pressure on her sensitive eardrums sent pain rippling through her. She pressed her face into the wood.

When she felt sure the danger had passed, Megan raised her head.

Clouds of smoke and dust clogged the air. Twisted bits of metal hung where the nearby swing bridge once stood. Coughing, she got to her feet, brushing off the girls, examining them for injuries.

Jillian's eyes grew wide as she pointed at Megan's right hand. "You cut yourself."

Blood dripped from a gash on the back of her right hand. She'd barely noticed. Megan forced a tremulous smile.

"It's okay, sweetie. Just a little ouch."

A large gray wolf bounded toward the dock, skidded to a halt. It stood motionless, its nostrils twitching. Amber eyes filled with menace, the wolf silently regarded her. Megan involuntarily took a step back, even though she knew the wolf's identity.

This wolf was large and impressive in his powerful bulk. Not like a Normal. More like another type of Draicon, but they were extremely rare and nearly as despised as Shadow Wolves.

Impossible. Gabriel came from a powerful Cajun family whose influence extended far into the Council of Draicon ruling over Shadow Wolf Island.

Gabriel shifted back into a man and waved a hand, clothing his naked body.

"Take them into the house. I'm going to investigate." After growling the order, he ran in the direction of the bridge.

In her upstairs bedroom, Megan helped the twins strip off their clothing as she examined them for stray shrapnel. Acid churned in her stomach as they dressed. If they had been hurt…

Both girls dogged her footsteps as she found a towel in the bathroom to rub dry her dampened hair. The girls looked up in fear as footsteps sounded, but they relaxed when Gabriel poked his head inside.

"Everyone okay?"

"Fine. What happened?" Hiding her distress, Megan put the damp towel on the rack. He must not know what they'd planned.

When they'd reached the boat dock earlier, Megan had found water and a hole in the little rowboat. Desperate, she'd decided to hot-wire the other boats, but upon checking the engines, she found someone had yanked out the batteries.

Gabriel came inside, flashed a reassuring smile. Megan couldn't read his expression as he glanced out the bathroom window. "Whoever blew up the bridge wanted to keep us here. The storm will be here by tonight."

"Someone's trying to trap us here, and there's a hurricane coming? Shouldn't we try to find some way to leave?"

If Gabriel got them off the island, she and the twins could make a break for it.

"Whoever did this didn't breach my defenses. He blew the bridge by rigging it with C-4 on the pilings." Gabriel's voice was hard, but laced with respect. "He can't get on the island."

"And we can't get off!"

"We can."

He seemed too calm.

"You have a magic carpet that'll fly us out?"

A rueful smile touched his mouth. "Something almost as good. Inflatable boats. But the bay's too choppy." He flicked his gaze to the girls. "Can they swim?"

Her heart sinking, Megan shook her head.

"Then I'm not risking it. Our chances are better riding it out here. You're safe for now. The storm is barely a hurricane and we'll not take the full brunt. Just some high winds and rain, and the houses are on concrete stilts to protect against tidal surges. We have propane generators and food."

Oh, this was so not what she wanted to hear. They needed to leave. But he was right. It would have to wait until the storm passed.

He frowned at her bleeding hand. "That needs cleaning."

Gabriel led Megan over to the sink. From one of the drawers he pulled out a bottle of peroxide and bag of cotton. He wet a large cotton ball and began gently wiping her hand. The laceration wasn't deep, but it stung. She ignored the pain, staring out the window. Clouds scuttled across the sky, blotching out the sun. No way off the island now. Emotions squeezed her insides, but she refused to surrender to fear.

Their earlier trepidation vanished, Jenny and Jillian roved through the spacious bathroom. Jillian spotted the faded yellow rubber duck Megan had left half-hidden by a towel. Her eager hands grabbed the toy.

"Look, Megan!"

Gabriel turned. His gaze darkened and he dropped the bloodied cotton ball. In two strides he was at Jillian's side. She cried out as he snatched the duck.

The fierce Enforcer threw the toy into the drawer and slammed it shut. His dark brows knit together. "You don't touch that again. Ever. Understand?"

The low, dangerous tone of his voice made Jillian's mouth tremble. She backed away, her blue eyes wide.

A protective streak rose in Megan as she stepped before Jillian, facing Gabriel. "Leave her alone. It's just a toy. What's the big deal?"

A dark fury etched his face. "It's not hers and she shouldn't touch it. No one ever touches it."

Dread curled in her stomach. "Who does it belong to?"

His jaw ground violently. "My niece Amelia." Now his furious gaze held hers. Amber eyes. Wolf eyes. "She was a Shadow, just like you."

Megan's heart thundered in her chest. She cradled her injured hand. Clouds darkening the sky cast his face into shadow. Didn't want to know, had to ask. Had to know…

"Was?" she whispered. "What happened to her?"

Gabriel's jaw tensed to granite. "I killed her."

Chapter 4

Last one.

Wind kicked up sand eddies, swirling on the ground. Gabriel lifted a heavy metal shutter, hooked it into place over the window and attached it.

He'd changed into shorts and a white muscle shirt for the arduous task of shuttering his vacation home. Sweat dripped down his temples. Gabriel swiped his damp brow with the back of one hand. His home now resembled a ghost house, the shutters reflecting the remaining rays of the late afternoon sun.

Megan and the twins were in the guest cottage on the bayside, where they all would ride out the storm. It was the safest house on the island. Gabriel needed to be alone for now, away from the horror in their eyes, the alarm shadowing their faces. Fear was good for them. Let them think he was as nasty as his reputation.

The thought sickened him.

He sagged against the shutter, feeling sun-warmed steel heat his skin. Closing his eyes, he saw Amelia's trusting face as he stood in the pool with her favorite bath toy as incentive for learning to swim. Heard her squeals of laughter as she finished splashing toward him, then grabbed the yellow rubber duck in her small fist.

"I got it, Uncle Gabriel! I'm like Ducky, I can swim now!" she'd yelled.

He'd laughed and swung her up in his arms, as Simone and Alex watched proudly.

The duck.

The yellow duck.

That damn…duck!

He hurled the hammer at the sand. Amelia deserved much better. Learning how to swim in the deep end, first dance, first kiss…

Thanks to him, she'd have none of that. She was only ten years old.

I'm sorry.

Gabriel fisted his trembling hands. The approaching hurricane echoed his turbulent emotions. Warmth spread through his body. Wolf clawed to the surface, stirred up by guilt, anger and self-loathing. Plucking at his shirt, he felt as if hundreds of ants crawled over his skin. He rubbed his chin, alarmed to find thick stubble. Gray fur replaced the light hairs dusting the back of his hands.

The first physical manifestation of his Change.

It had grown more powerful since Raphael's mate had infused him with power during a vicious Morph fight. His sister-in-law Emily's touch had heightened his Draicon's magick. It had tripled Gabriel's powers, but also made his wolf more ferocious.

The hell with it. He allowed the wolf to flow through him. Muscles rippled and stretched, bones lengthened. He snarled at the elements, feeling the primitive need to rip and tear and destroy.

The sweet vanilla scent of childhood halted the process.

Gabriel stiffened, fisting his hands/paws. Acute senses warned that a twin stood behind him on the deck. His human side wrestled for control. Even though the wolf would never hurt an innocent, he could not allow a young one to witness his transformation.

"Mr. Gabriel?"

"Go away, Jillian." His voice was a low whip-lash, hinting of danger.

"Are you still mad at me?"

Closing his eyes, he breathed deeply.

"I'm sorry I touched your toy, Mr. Gabriel."

"I'm not mad at you, Jillian."

He managed to corral the violent emotions. Gabriel studied his hands, relieved to see they were normal. The wolf was gone. For now.

"You can call me Jilly. Everyone does."

He turned, wondering if this young one would know how close she'd danced to the knife's edge of violence.

"I'm not afraid of you." A frown dented her brow. "I'm worried about you. You hurt."

At his blank stare, she rubbed her thin chest. "In here."

Tension knotted the spot she'd indicated. "I'm fine," he lied.

"No, you're not," she said seriously. "I can tell. I can feel inside you. You don't want anyone to know because you don't like what happens when you feel this way."

Merde, a seven-year-old could tell? Gabriel retrieved the hammer. As he brushed it free of sand, he glanced at the solemn girl examining the inside of his canvas tool bag.

"You can feel inside me?"

She nodded. Seldom had he used his enormous powers of mind control to delve into a child's thoughts. Children were innocent and their motivations and thought patterns as clear as shiny glass. They were easy to read, but he hated having to do it.

He motioned to the steps, and when she'd sat beside him, he turned the hammer over in his hand. "Can you read other people's thoughts?"

Jillian gave him a guileless look. "Only if they allow me to, or if they're so loud they're screaming at me. Like they're yelling out loud, but they're not. Gram taught me not to be rude and invade their minds."

In a ladylike gesture, she folded her hands in her lap. "I tried once, when my friend Andrea bragged her hair was prettier than mine. I went into her mind to see the truth. She hated her hair and I told her so. Megan punished me and made me apologize. She said it was wrong. I didn't mean to hurt Andrea and I promised never to do it again."

"Megan is right. Using power holds you accountable for your magick."

Gabriel sucked in a deep breath. "When you get older, you'll understand the difference between doing it for the right reasons or just to be a bully. You'll learn to shut out others' thoughts, too, so you can have peace."

How he wished he could experience such peace. Hadn't, not since Amelia and Simone had died.

"You didn't do it, Mr. Gabriel. You didn't kill her."

"What?"

"Amelia. You said you killed her, but I felt

what you felt." Jillian shook her head. "You're not like the bad men who hurt Shadows."

A fist of guilt and alarm squeezed his throat. "What bad men, Jilly?"

"The men on the island who wanted to hurt Megan. The fisherman on the boat who hit her, and wanted to do the same things the bad men wanted." She looked confused. "I didn't understand. Why did they want to take her clothes off?"

His wolf silently howled in protective rage. Gabriel forced it down. Going hog wild on his emotions wouldn't help her now. He mustered all his control and turned to look Jillian in the eye.

"There are bad men who do things like that, little one. They aren't nice and you need to stay away from them. There is a blackness inside their hearts and their spirits."

For a moment they sat in silence on the steps, staring at the gathering storm clouds. Sandpipers and seagulls flew toward the mainland. Jillian looked worried.

"Is it going to be a bad storm, Mr. Gabriel?" she whispered.

He gave her a reassuring smile. "Call me Gabriel. No *Mister*. Naw, we'll just see a bit of wind and rain. I can feel it in my bones. You'll be safe."

She chatted about the storms she'd experienced on her island. Gabriel listened, paying attention the way few adults did. He liked kids. He'd always been good with his brother Etienne's four children…and Alex's Amelia. He'd longed for children, but didn't dare procreate with his bad genes. Gabriel's chest felt hollow. Never would he want a son or daughter to endure the shame and aversion he had known in childhood.

"What's this?"

Fascination stole over her face as she stared at the blue-inked scrolling on his left bicep. She traced it with a finger.

"You got marked, too. Did it hurt like cousin Megan's?"

The attention span of the young.

"It's a tattoo, Jilly. My brother Indigo put it there for me. It means 'fierce one' in the Old Language of our ancestors."

"It's pretty. Megan's mark is just numbers.

She cried after it was done. She tried not to let us hear, but I knew she was crying."

"Numbers? Where?"

"On the back of her neck, like female Shadow Wolves get when they turn twenty-one."

So now they were inking all Shadows to keep track of them? His gorge rose. Wolf growled to the surface, driven by the urge to protect and defend his Megan.

His?

The notion stunned him. Megan Moraine was a Shadow Wolf who needed escorting to a safe house. Yet his emotions were that of a bonded male for his draicara.

Jillian sighed. "I guess they'll give me one when I get older, too."

Her practical tone sent chills through him. Gabriel took her hand and gave it a reassuring squeeze.

He started to say no.

Words died on his tongue, a promise he wanted to give her, but couldn't. She looked so trusting, his heart twisted. Once he'd made the same promise to another child, and failed.

He couldn't promise anything to children. Not anymore.

He enlisted her help in picking up his tools. Gabriel let Jillian proudly carry the hammer and screwdriver while he took the canvas tool bag.

When they reached the guest house, Megan was sitting on a deck chair. Her legs were tucked beneath her as she combed her hair, gazing at the whitecaps crashing against the barnacle-riddled seawall.

She began to sing. The purity of her voice reminded him of sunrise over the bayou. It soothed him, brought the beast to a standstill. His entire body tingled with the desire to draw close, sit at her feet and let her voice wash over him in a cleansing flood. Music was his balm, a necessity to tame his wolf.

Then Jennifer burst out of the house, a tiny, pink-clad whirlwind waving a small conch shell. Megan held the seashell to her ear.

Gabriel stared. Not classically pretty, Megan had an exotic, Fey beauty. Her cheeks were stained pink by the rising breeze, long hair wreathing her heart-shaped face. Her mouth was cherry-red and moist. A blue T-shirt molded to firm, round breasts.

The unabashed laughter in her sea-blue eyes lured him like a sailor to a siren's deadly song. Megan laughed, the sound pure enjoyment.

All his senses focused on her, his hands shaking with longing. He wanted a piece of that honest happiness, if only for a fleeting moment. Not the joking front he showed to disguise his real emotions. Gabriel yearned for something as simple as the joy of sharing a seashell's whispers.

He hadn't experienced that since…when?

Since Amelia died three years ago. When his niece died, a light of innocence in his life had winked out. His niece had adored him, and she'd known exactly what he was. And still, she wasn't afraid of him.

Jillian set down the hammer and screwdriver and scampered up the steps. A shrill of laughter echoed through the air as she held the seashell to her ear. He felt as if he'd invaded a special and private moment between Megan and her cousins. A lead weight settled on his chest as he went to stash his tools in the shed.

The incoming storm sent a vibrating hum through his tensed body. Wolf howled to release the pent-up emotions. Gabriel glanced backward. Megan and the twins could not see him.

Sand stung his cheeks. He relished the wind slapping his face.

The hell with it. No longer able to hold back his internal storm, Gabriel shape-shifted.

Gabriel was running wild.

Megan's heart thundered in her chest as she watched a large gray wolf race back and forth on the beach. The wolf's raw power and dark intensity sent a chill down her spine. Larger than most, muscles rippled under the lupine's gray fur.

He could break her spine with one lunge. She wrapped her arms around herself, sinking back into the cover of the mangroves.

She'd come to the beach to tell him about the silver-haired man blowing up the bridge in hopes he'd mention where the inflatable boats were stashed.

Megan peered around the mangroves, her palms growing cold and sweaty. What if Gabriel suddenly turned on them? She'd glimpsed his haunted look when he'd left to shutter the houses. But this wolf was not vulnerable. This wolf could tear and kill and destroy.

Never had she seen such a display, as if the wolf released all the emotions the man could not. This wolf snapped at the surf. It tipped back its head and released a long, mournful howl that echoed the cadence of the crashing surf.

The wolf was wild and dangerous.

A delicious scent of pine, leather and sweet wine drifted on the wind. It overwhelmed her senses. Megan closed her eyes, overcome with the sensuality calling to her. No wolf she had ever known emitted such an enticing scent.

The idea hit her like a resounding slap on the face. Shadows didn't do that. From what little she knew, neither did Normals.

Ferals did.

Panic squeezed her throat. Ferals were wild and unpredictable. Their blood ran thick with the instinct to hunt, kill and mate. Male Ferals were dominating, highly sexual and aggressive. Their scents were strong and irresistible to females. When a male saw a female he wanted, the Feral Draicon pursued with ruthless determination until he had her naked and submissive beneath his powerful body. Their blood ran thick with passion and animalistic need.

Yet as she watched Gabriel, doubt laced through the fear. He'd seemed gentle and protective of the twins. Even when he was furious over the rubber duck, he'd left instead of raging at Jillian.

As wild as the wolf acted, the man acted restrained. How could Gabriel be a Feral since he was an Enforcer? The Council of Draicon executed vicious Ferals and sent others to demon prisons. As despised as Shadows were, Ferals were hated more. Their ability to blend in with the human populace was limited by their savage animal nature, often triggered by sexual arousal and heightened emotions.

Once the most dangerous Ferals were called Trans-Ferals. Long ago, they'd been hunted to extinction.

Megan felt a tug of empathy for Feral Draicon. As a Shadow, she wanted equality among all their species.

A savage beauty reflected in the wolf's running with the wind. Her heart thundered again, echoing the cadence of distant crashing thunder. Her pulse raced with excitement.

How she longed to run wild, heedless of watchful Draicon ready to punish her for shifting into a wolf. Megan took one step forward, her body thrumming with anticipation.

The wolf skidded, his big paws digging into the wet sand. He pivoted, his huge head swerving in her direction, focused on her with a predatory look.

Wild amber eyes met hers.

The wolf was king. If he wanted, the wolf could track her scent, have her on the ground before she could escape.

Though her heart pounded hard, Megan held her position. She returned the wolf's dominating look. She blinked, and the wolf was gone, replaced by a man wearing a white shirt and khaki shorts.

Gabriel.

Sea mist dampened his dark hair. His muscled body was hard with sexual aggression. He stalked toward her with determined purpose.

Afraid of his power, she stood her ground. Megan refused to lower her gaze as other Draicon would do facing a predator.

"I can smell your fear. I told you before, I won't hurt you," he said softly. "How long have you been watching?"

"I just got here," she admitted. "It was fascinating watching you as a wolf. I can't remember how long it's been since I saw a Draicon shift and we're prohibited from shifting into wolves on Shadow Island."

"Why can't you shift?"

"I guess they're afraid we'll become more powerful as invisible wolves than invisible in our human form."

Raw sexuality radiated from him. Megan swallowed hard. "I didn't come to spy on you. I came looking for you to tell you something."

He stopped close enough for her to smell his delicious maleness mingling with evergreen and rain. Passion filled his heated gaze. His nostrils flared as if he'd caught her scent. A pulse hammered at the base of his throat.

"Tell me what, *chère?*"

Though she was still untouched, Megan

sensed his desire. He wanted her, badly. And animal instinct fought for control of the man. Something inside her clawed to the surface, wanting him just as badly.

Gabriel unclenched his fists. He caught her hand in his and turned it over. The gentleness of the gesture contrasted sharply to his earlier display of brute strength. He ran a thumb over her cut.

"It's starting to heal already. Good." He dropped her hand and traced a line along her jaw. His touch was gentle, but she instinctively recognized the possessiveness.

A wolf marking his territory.

"Tell you…" She halted, shuddering with pleasure as he stroked a line down the sensitive curve of her neck.

He dropped his hands. "Go back to the cottage. The storm's getting closer and the twins will be scared."

"Why are you so concerned when all you'll do is turn them over to the authorities? For all the stories I've heard about you…"

He swore softly, his expression growing

cold and dangerous. "I'm not what you think, Megan. Don't underestimate me."

As he started to push past her, she blurted out, "I know who blew up the bridge. I think it was the same man from the restaurant, a man with silver hair."

"Why are you telling me now? Why not before?"

"We're stuck here together and I need your help getting off this island. If this man is determined to trap us, can we leave? You said you had other boats. Are they nearby?"

"What were you and the girls doing on the dock?"

Softness laced the steely words. When she didn't answer, he stepped behind her and placed his palms on her shoulders. His touch was gentle, but she sensed his determination. He would have answers.

"I told you, you're safe here. I won't hurt you." His fingers began to knead her muscles, sending delicious heat spiraling through her body. Earlier tension evaporated, replaced by sensual need. Her head tilted back like a sunflower seeking warmth.

Gabriel wrapped his arms around her waist. Power was in those strong limbs. He bent his head, warm breath feathering over her cheek.

"Tell me, Megan."

"The boats were useless, anyway." She trembled with sudden need.

"I know. I disabled them to keep you here." She quivered with anticipation as his mouth nuzzled her neck.

Struggling to keep her thoughts straight, Megan stiffened. "Hope you didn't disable the inflatables, too. Where are they?"

"In a safe place, *chère*."

"Are you sure? Maybe I can help you secure them before the storm." A low moan escaped her as his fingers stroked over the sides of her neck.

"No."

His hands anchored her to him. His hard male body was filled with enormous power. Yet the hands now splayed over her belly were gentle and his lips tracing a line down to her collarbone were soft and warm.

A different hardness pressed into her backside. A whimper of erotic pleasure tore from her throat as his hands drifted lower, palming her lower belly, pressing her against his erection.

A vision arose in her mind. She was naked on all fours as Gabriel knelt behind her, his large hands on her hips, his face etched with ruthless intent as he took her in the traditional position of a wolf claiming its mate....

Megan slammed a door on the image. *Never.*

Trying to regain her lost composure, she jerked out of his embrace. How could she feel this way about her jailer?

"Stop doing this to me," she whispered.

Amber burned in his dark eyes. "Doing what, *chère?*"

"Making me want you. The vision you put in my mind, me, you, naked together."

A muscle clenched in his taut jaw. "That wasn't me."

Stunned, she stared. "How can I know you're not manipulating me? You're not forcing me to feel like this?"

"I wouldn't," he said quietly. "I may be many things, but I'd never force you mentally or any other way. Megan, you have nothing to fear from me. Soon, you will come to trust in that."

"I've had others tell me the same. Why should I believe you won't hurt me, Enforcer?"

"Because when I find the one who left those bruises, and I will find him, I'll do this to him or anyone else who dares to touch you."

He plucked out a heavy paving stone from the pathway. A chill raced down her spine as he crushed it in one hand. Caught by the increasing wind, the powder blew away.

"I don't make promises I can't keep, not anymore. But I will promise you this. That sonofabitch will pay for your pain."

Gabriel dusted off his hands and jogged away.

Numb with shock, she stared at the missing paver. Gabriel was no ordinary Draicon. He was more than a dangerous adversary. He was lethal to anyone opposing him.

Who was Gabriel Robichaux and what secrets did he hide?

Chapter 5

As night fell, the hurricane began battering the tiny island. Wind whistled through the trees and thunder crackled and boomed.

Megan let out a small gasp as a thick branch hit the roof. The news magazine she'd been reading fell to the couch beside her.

Lying on the floor, Gabriel looked up from the board game he played with Jillian and Jennifer. He felt her anxiety as if she'd telegraphed it, just as he'd felt it on the beach when she'd seen him run as wolf. Stupid of him to release his beast, but fortunately Megan had little contact with Draicon.

She could never guess his secret.

"Don't worry, *chère*. This cottage, she's built like a tank."

After the rain began, trepidation replaced the twins' excitement about the oncoming storm. He'd coaxed them to help cook one of his Cajun specialties. After dinner he taught them Wii bowling.

Now he was successfully losing at Monopoly.

"The roof on our house leaks so much that we can't sleep because all our beds get soaked. I patched it with tarps and duct tape, but it didn't help. Still, it's better than sleeping out on the beach," Megan told him.

He could feel his wolf clawing to the surface. Gabriel tipped his cowboy hat down, hiding the telltale flash in his eyes.

Your eyes, oh Gabriel, what's happening with your eyes?

"Duct tape? Not a hammer and roofing nails?" He rolled the dice.

"Shadows aren't permitted anything that can be used as a weapon. If you want something fixed, you put your name on a waiting list for a licensed repairman. It's a very long list, unless you pay a lot of money to have your name moved up."

"When did this start?"

Megan frowned. "When Governor Sacks changed the rules four years ago. He wasn't so bad before. I guess he got greedy, seeing the chance to make a profit as he split bribes with licensed repairmen. And…other things."

He moved his car token on the board to Jillian's smug smile. "Boardwalk," she crowed, holding out her hand. "Ten hundred million dollars, please."

"You're a very demanding landlord."

"Someone has to pay to get our roof fixed," Jennifer told him.

Gabriel shelled out the correct amount of bills to Jillian. "Have you gone through official channels and filed a formal complaint with the council?"

"Those fools? Shadows have no rights," Megan said as she thumbed through the magazine. "No books or magazines, either. Nothing to read, except what we can buy on the black market."

"What do you do for fun?"

A yearning entered her blue eyes. "We're too busy moving for fun. I've always dreamed of having a real home like this." Megan tossed aside the magazine. "It's just a dream. Maybe, someday."

Jennifer rolled and selected a card from the stack. Her face wrinkled as she studied the words and she scrambled to her feet. "Megan, what does it say?"

"It's a Get out of Jail Free card. Save it, sweetie. Very valuable."

"Jenny, can't you read?" he asked.

"A little. Megan teaches us, even though she's not supposed to." Jennifer clapped a hand over her mouth. "I'm not supposed to say. If anyone finds out, they'll punish us. Shadows can't go to school."

Megan tensed until Gabriel offered a small smile. "It's okay, Jenny. I won't tell."

Still, she didn't lose her wariness. She reminded him of a wild animal caught in a trap. Megan shifted, the move accentuating the thrust of her breasts against the T-shirt. There was nothing overtly sexual about it, yet he felt a hard kick of desire.

Gabriel stretched out his long legs. For years he'd dealt with female Shadows without any intense reaction. When he'd seen her on the beach, his wolf wanted to mark her as his own. The urge overrode common sense.

Around Megan, he'd nearly lost control. It was almost as if she was…

She couldn't be his destined mate. Long ago, he'd thought the same of another woman and it had landed him in trouble. He stopped seeking emotional intimacy. Still, he sent a gentle probe into her mind, testing to see if the bond was there. When he met a blank wall, he felt a curious mixture of relief and disappointment.

He didn't want a destined mate, who would hold the missing half of his magick. Hell, bonding with him was lethal. Most Draicon yearned to find their mates and exchange powers during a sexual mating lock. But how could he share his powers and turn his mate into something dark and dangerous?

His brothers had mates and even Alex was dating again. Gabriel quietly resigned himself to being alone forever. Sometimes the loneliness was a crushing weight, but it was better for all.

The rain finally eased and the crashes of thunder moved away. When the girls began yawning, Megan glanced at the clock on the fireplace mantel.

"Time for bed," she told them.

Gabriel stood, scooped a twin under each arm as his hat tumbled to the floor. They giggled as he jogged to the back bedroom. It had single beds with clean white sheets turned down for the night.

"Gabriel, can you read us a story?" Jenny called.

At the doorway, he stared at the cozy scene of two identical girls dressed in green pajamas sitting in their beds. A lump lodged in his throat. Amelia, the red ribbon in her curls matching her candy-striped pajamas. Expectation dancing on her face as she held out her favorite storybook. Alex mock-punching him in the arm. "Go on, Gabe, read to her. Good practice for when you become a father."

Shaking the vision free, he forced a smile. "Megan should do it."

With exact control, he headed into the kitchen. Cooking always made him feel human. Gabriel washed sweet peppers and onions and set them aside. A frown touched his brow as he scanned his prize collection of knives.

The butcher knife was missing.

A delicate floral scent drifted into the kitchen. Gabriel faced the doorway. Light gleamed off the sharp steel blade in Megan's hand. Her entire body tensed like a stretched rubber band. The acid stench of her fear swam in his nostrils.

"Come toward me slowly with your hands raised. No shifting, no quick moves. I can shift into Shadow and stab you before you know what hit you."

"Do you really want to hurt me, *chère?*"

"Shut up." She gestured with the butcher knife. "Over there, by the fridge."

He moved slowly as to not alarm her.

"Now put your hands behind you."

When she took out several zip ties from her pocket, he had to admire her inventiveness. "Take those from my tool bag?"

Suddenly she vanished. Gabriel jerked his head around.

She was gone.

He felt a prick at his throat, then something

slip around his wrists, looping to the fridge doors behind him.

A voice spoke close to his ear. "Jillian did. Why do you think she went looking for you?"

"Using a child to do something this deceptive. Ah, Megan, I'm disappointed." He didn't bother to test the cuffs. If needed, he could break free in a heartbeat. Instead, he tracked her scent to the counter and watched her reappear. In her hands she held a heavy silver fork wrapped in a dish towel. Megan slid the fork between the cufflinks and his hands and tossed the towel aside.

"The cuffs won't hold you, but the silver will drain your powers."

No, he thought. It took more than a fork to affect his kind. More like a cafeteria filled with silver.

"Why now, Megan? Why not try before the hurricane?"

"I told you, the girls can't swim and I'm not risking their lives. I'll do whatever I can to keep them safe. They're all I have, understand? And you're not going to hurt them, and neither is anyone else. They deserve a life."

The vulnerability shadowing her face turned his heart over. "And you don't? What about your needs, Megan?"

She dragged in a tremulous breath. "I just want to save them. It's too late for me," she whispered.

Gabriel's guts clenched. "You're only twenty-six. So much pain I see inside your eyes. Who hurt you, *chère?* Who hurt you this badly?"

Her lower lip wobbled. Her thoughts flashed bright as a sun flare. *I can't trust anyone. No one gives a damn about me.*

A fierce scowl tightened her face. "Stop doing that. You know, reading my mind."

"Can't help it. Your thoughts are like a tiger prowling in the bayou. They stand out."

Immediately he got an image of a brick wall. Megan turned ashen as Gabriel silently cursed. He had to win her trust. He sent her a reassuring image of a waterfall surrounded by children laughing and frolicking. For an instant, the bricks slowly toppled downward, as if hit by a heavy sledgehammer. He seized his chance and locked her mind to his, forcing his thoughts upon her.

Don't be afraid.

Go away. The thought was shrill inside his head.

You know these won't hold me. I can snap out of them before you make it to the kitchen door. C'mon chère, *work with me. I promise you, I'll keep you safe.*

I'm a fool if I believe you.

Do you really think I'd let you risk your life in this storm? I'd cut my own throat with that knife before I allowed that to happen, because I vowed to always take care of my own.

That thought startled the *hell* out of him. Gabriel went still, shocked by the fierce declaration. A nagging suspicion flared. Megan was an assignment. A Shadow needing help. Yet he'd never felt such intensity. Not even with the woman who'd run from him screaming a full century before.

"Take these cuffs off," he urged.

"No." She backed away, the knife lowered. She was feeling the shock, as well.

Gabriel tried for humor. "I could rip off the doors to free myself, but *chère,* this fridge, Alex is still paying for it and he'd kill me."

"Please, don't make me do this." The plea was a faint whisper. The knife clattered to the tile floor, echoing in the sudden silence.

His heart thudded against his chest. When her thoughts surfaced, Gabriel seized the moment. The strong ties binding his wrist snapped like thread. He stepped forward, staring down into her eyes.

He pulled her into his arms. She went without resistance. She felt good, soft and giving, and yet her femininity hid a core of steel.

Steel forged by hellfire, by pain. If he could, he'd remove her pain.

Cupping her face in his warm palms, he kissed her gently, oh so gently. Megan's eyes closed. Encouraged, he deepened the kiss.

A shock surged through him, as if electrical current sizzled through the fusing contact of their mouths. It made any kiss he'd ever experienced feel tame. Jerking away, Megan rubbed her mouth. Shock dawned in her eyes.

"No," she whispered.

"Yes," he breathed. He slid a trembling hand around the nape of her neck, pulled her forward and kissed her again.

This time, she clutched his shoulders, nails digging into his shirt. Pleasure and pain mingled as he swept his tongue inside her mouth, seeking, finding, holding her. Claiming her with his mouth, staking his mark on her. Her soft, pliant body trembled as he reversed positions and pushed her against the cool, hard steel. He felt her breasts and their pearl-hard nipples press against him as she drank in his mouth. She smelled warm and sweet, and he inhaled deeply, drawing her scent into his lungs.

Beneath the urgent pressure of his mouth, Megan made a low sound. He released her, panting raggedly, staring into the dark blueness of eyes shining with confusion and desire.

Gabriel fisted his hands as thunder suddenly crashed and wind pushed against the tight enclosure of the shutters.

Megan was no ordinary Shadow.

She was his destined mate. The female he was to bond with, who would know all his intimate secrets as she knew his body.

He was in deep trouble.

Chapter 6

Her draicaron, her destined mate, was an Enforcer?

Megan wiped her kiss-swollen mouth with a shaking hand. "Get out," she said in a dull voice.

Amber flashed in his eyes as he reached out to her. His hand dropped. Wordlessly he stalked out of the kitchen.

She sagged down to the tile floor and slammed a fist against her thigh, trying to escape the sensual memory of his hot kiss. If Gabriel were cruel, she'd sense it. He'd shown nothing but kindness and consideration since their capture.

Megan scented pine and rain and glanced up.

Gabriel stood in the doorway. A key dangled from his fingers.

"The shed is in the back."

Confused, she scrambled to her feet. "You're an Enforcer and you're letting me go? How can I trust you?"

"You have little choice. And I'm not letting you go." He went to her, opened her palm, dropped the key inside. "This is yours for safe-keeping, to show you I mean no harm. I'm here to help you, Megan."

"You can't be my destined mate." She gave a brittle laugh like cracked glass. "You stand for everything I hate about Draicon. You capture my people and enforce laws that bind us."

"That's what you've been told." He clasped his hands around her closed palm. "The stories precede me. Is any one of us who he appears to be?"

"Who are you?"

He tensed, and she felt a surge of his power. "Someone who will get you to safety. And not just because you're mine."

"I'm not yours," she protested, pocketing the key.

Gabriel leaned closer, pinning her against the

refrigerator. He cupped her face in his hands. "Yes, you are."

This time his kiss was warm and authoritative, his mouth possessing her. Megan sighed as he coaxed her to open to him.

If she wasn't careful, this dangerous Draicon could creep into her heart. She had longed for love and acceptance, but how could she share a life with a man who detested her race?

"You're still innocent," he murmured, breaking the kiss. "Good. I don't think I'd deal kindly with any man who came before me."

"How can you tell?"

He gave her a sensual look that made the space between her legs throb wildly. "Your scent. It's delicious, layered with traces of wildflowers and honey. I can't smell another male."

Now her cheeks began to burn. "I saved myself for someone I loved. Not a destined mate." *Someone who can love me for who I am.*

Gabriel ran a thumb across her flushed cheek. "You can't fight instinct. When the time comes, I'll treat you right."

"You're talking as you'll be my first."

"I will be," he said softly. "But now isn't the

time. We have to get you and the girls out of here. Right before dawn, when it's still dark, we'll leave."

"I can't risk it," she protested. "This is all too much, too confusing. I have to protect the girls, I made a promise and nothing will stop me from keeping it. What will you do, beg for clemency from the council just because I'm your destined mate? Or will you turn me over anyway?"

Silence dripped between them.

"I can't trust you, Gabriel, just because suddenly, oh, we're destined mates and everything will be fine. You say you're going to keep us safe. How? If you expect me to follow your orders, then you have to be honest with me."

Emotions warred in his eyes. Gabriel shoved a hand through his thick, ragged hair. "Okay, Megan. In the morning, I'll tell you the truth."

"Why not now?"

He passed a hand over her face and she felt her eyes closing. "Time for you to sleep."

She felt warm in his arms as he carried her to bed. Gabriel settled her between the covers. He hated giving her a mental push, but she needed rest and in her pent-up state, she'd never sleep.

Loathe to leave her, he stretched out on the bed, making sure to keep his distance.

When he awoke, wolf senses warned dawn was not far off. Gabriel stood and stretched his long arms, then paced over to the shuttered window. The rain had stopped. He snapped on a light.

Megan awoke to a gentle whisper in her ear. He longed to touch her, but didn't dare, knowing how fiercely the animal inside him wanted to mount her.

Her mouth was parted and sexy. That mouth could drive a man crazy with lust.

"Please don't do that again," she rumbled in a sexy, sleep-laden voice.

"Do what?"

"Put me to sleep." She sat up, rubbing her head. "It leaves me feeling out of sorts, like a sleeping pill hangover. I'm sensitive to those things."

He waited while she showered and changed. When she emerged into the bedroom, the knife present in his heart since Amelia's death twisted a little.

Pacing back and forth, he jammed his hands into his jeans pockets. Telling her risked everything. But he knew Megan needed the truth to follow him.

She'd told him as much.

"I'm not what I seem." He flinched at her wary look. "I'm an Enforcer, hired by the council to bring in Shadows. That's my cover. I use it while escorting the Shadows to safe houses and arranging for the next escort until they can reach my brother in New Orleans. Alex then gives them new identities and lives."

The truth felt good. "I'm in charge of an elaborate underground railroad. I use the Enforcer role to assist Shadows. I don't hurt them. I help Shadows escape."

Megan's lovely mouth opened and closed. She glanced at the doorway and her eyes widened. "Little pitchers."

A jerk of her thumb. His blood pressure plummeted.

Merde.

The twins came out of Shadow. "I knew it," Jenny crowed. "I knew you weren't a bad man, even before Jilly told me."

"I knew it first," Jillian protested.

Gabriel's eyes narrowed. "How long have you been eavesdropping?"

Jillian's lower lip trembled. Jennifer fidgeted with her hands and stared at the floor.

"We were just playing hide-and-seek and saw you and Megan were awake, so we wanted to come in," Jennifer finally admitted.

"But you didn't. You kept yourself in Shadow," Megan pointed out.

"Never do that again. There are some things adults talk about that aren't meant for children," Gabriel admonished.

"I'm sorry," both girls echoed.

Megan frowned. "You know this means punishment. No bedtime stories for two nights."

The twins looked crestfallen and began to plead for their favorite entertainment. Gabriel silenced them with a look.

He went to them, hunkered down to their level. "Listen to me, Jilly, Jenny. What you overheard, you must keep secret. Understand? It's very important."

"Okay," they both said.

"Go clean up and get ready for breakfast."

They trudged away.

Megan scooted off the bed as he closed the door. She lowered her voice. "I don't understand. How can you keep up such a complicated cover? What about the stories about you torturing Shadows? What about the council? Don't they demand to see proof the Shadows are back on the island?"

His gaze went flat. "Not when I bring them proof of their demise. They don't care if the Shadows are alive or dead, so dead is just as good to them. When Alex gives them new identities, I take their clothing, spill their blood on it and present it to the council. I collect the bounty on their heads and use the money to fund more escapes and the safe houses."

"The stories..." As awareness dawned on her face. "You plant the stories as a cover, too."

"After they're safe, I give them a mental push. They don't remember anything except I'm the bad guy."

Large blue eyes met his. "I sense you're telling the truth. It feels right. But I also sense you don't feel comfortable with this."

"The truth can be a weapon in the wrong

hands. It was a gamble telling you, and now that the girls know…damn. We have to make sure all this is kept just to ourselves."

He hated revealing himself. Gabriel felt as if someone had stripped off a layer of clothing. But he had no choice when it came to gaining her trust.

"Thank you." Gratitude shone in her eyes. She looked at him as if he were a knight in shining armor instead of what he truly was: a dangerous wolf. The family muscle, whom they used when they needed to prowl and attack Morphs.

The family shame, hidden away.

He stared at her with longing, wanting to hand over the moon on a stainless steel platter if it meant she looked at him again like that. As if he were normal and not a Draicon to be feared.

Megan stepped closer to him. "I understand. I have something I must share with you, when the time is right. I will tell you this now. I was headed for New Orleans."

Startled, he blinked hard. "The city of the Draicon council? Right into the wolves' lair? What for?"

"It involves finding a relative. I didn't give

details to the girls because I hate raising their hopes and watching them get crushed." Her lower lip wobbled tremulously. "Too many times they've been crushed in the past."

"Hey, there," he said gently, cupping her cheek, unable to prevent from touching her. "It will all work out, *chère*. I'm on your side."

Her skin felt like smooth silk beneath his calloused fingertips. Gabriel felt his wolf surface. He touched a corner of her mouth with his, drew back with satisfaction at her flare of arousal.

When her fingers traced his bottom lip, he groaned. Sweet tension sang through his body. Gabriel closed his eyes, summoning all his control.

He opened his eyes. "Time enough later for play. Get ready and be downstairs so we can move out in half an hour."

Sexual need pumped through his blood as she trailed her finger down to his broad chest. "Are you better at love play than Monopoly?"

Arousal flared on her face as he took her finger, pressed it against his mouth and gave it a long, slow lick. "Don't test me, darling, not in the bedroom. Because it's a game you will lose. And I'll make sure it's a long, slow surrender where you scream with pleasure. All night long."

Chapter 7

Ribbons of rose and gold drifted over the leaden sky. Megan's heart lurched in her chest as Gabriel paddled across the bay.

They'd gotten off to a late start because of the twins dragging their feet. Now, instead of having the waters to themselves, they shared the bay with three other boats.

The hearty breakfast he'd insisted on them eating felt like a bowling ball in her stomach. She spread out her hands, keeping up the cover of Shadow. Cloaked like this, their little group could see each other in the boat, but others could not.

Shadowing herself was easy, but cloaking an entire boat and its occupants took all her concentration. The silver-haired man wasn't in sight, but she could feel him out there, waiting to strike. Was he another Enforcer, eager to take in prey?

I don't know.

Gabriel's telepathic thoughts entered her mind. She found the sensation thrilling and a little intimidating.

When they finally made it to the mainland, Gabriel tied up the boat and hefted himself onto the dock. He paused at a piling, and snagged a set of keys off a rusty nail.

She kept up the cover of Shadow as they walked to the parking lot. Gabriel unlocked a white minivan.

Jillian handed him a black Stetson exactly like the one he'd left behind, except this one looked less faded from the sun. "Here's your hat, Gabriel."

He thanked her and clapped it on his head. Gabriel started the van and pulled out of the parking lot.

"Where are you taking us?"

"North. There's a safe house near Orlando.

Daniel will take good care of you and the twins."

"I thought you were taking us to New Orleans."

"I will. But I need to check out a few things along the way."

Laced through his casual tone was an undercurrent of something. She didn't like secrets, either keeping them or having someone keep them from her.

"What things? What's wrong?"

He drummed his fingers on the steering wheel. "Just something I need to check. We'll stop there for lunch, for you to replenish your energy." He gave her a pointed look. "Unless you want to replenish it a different way."

Crimson ignited her cheeks. Draicon required energy to perform magick, and usually siphoned it either from eating rare meat or engaging in vigorous sex.

"A hamburger will do me just fine," she replied.

"Too bad," he murmured.

Jillian piped up from the backseat. "Why do you wear that cowboy hat, Gabriel?"

"Keeps my brains stuffed inside my head, little one." He grinned at her in the mirror as Jillian made a face. "Naw, I wear it because it keeps me centered on what's really important. Home, family, who I am. A Cajun at heart."

Megan studied his T-shirt logo. "The Blazin Cajun. I've heard of that restaurant chain, even though I've only been in the States once when I was little, long before Shadows became imprisoned on the island. My cousin Sissy told me it was her favorite. She loved their magma sauce. Have you ever had their food?"

"Sometimes." He glanced at her. "When I cook it myself. I own the chain."

Her eyes went wide. "All ten restaurants?"

He nodded.

They weren't on the road more than fifteen minutes when Gabriel glanced at the dashboard and muttered something in Cajun French. She leaned over and her heart sank. The gas gauge was nearly on *E*.

"Jay forgot to fill the tank. We have to stop."

Megan looked out the window, trying not to worry. She'd had a pointed talk with the twins about the importance of keeping Gabriel's secret. As long as they stayed in the van, they should be…

"Megan, I have to go," Jennifer piped up.

"I told you to go before you left the house," Megan repeated.

"I didn't have to go then," her cousin said with the aggravating logic of a seven-year-old.

"It's okay, little one," Gabriel soothed. "There's a gas station up ahead. Let Megan take you inside, you and your sister."

Jillian protested she didn't have to go. Gabriel shot her a look in the mirror. "I'm not stopping again."

The bathroom was dingy, but clean. When the girls finished and washed their hands, Megan stared at the fly-specked mirror. Lost in thought, she studied her reflection. The purple shadows on her face were gone, pink flushed her cheeks and a sparkle replaced the dull wariness in her eyes.

Had Gabriel done that?

Megan examined a streak of blond showing through the blackness of her hair. The hair dye was leeching out her identity. Bracing her hands on either side of the sink, she gazed at her reflection. Who was she? Shadow? Draicon? She was Halfling, a combination of both. It was important she blend into this world if she were to survive.

Draicon shifted into wolves easily. It had been so long. Megan longed to try.

Jenny and Jillian grew restless and shuffled around. She motioned to them. "Go back to the van. I'll meet you there."

In the bathroom with the door locked, she concentrated. Megan fisted her hands, willing the wildness to surface. It was crazy, risking it like this, but the impulse could not be curbed.

"Please, oh, please. Just once," she whispered. It had been ten years since she'd become wolf.

Iridescent sparks of blue and red, not the normal spectral trail that Draicon emitted, filled the air. Megan felt her body shimmer and ache.

The Change was happening.

Fur grew on the back of her hands. She grit her teeth, remembered the animal inside her and willed it out.

Her hands turned into large paws. Gray fur

rippled along her arms, but the rest of her body refused to cooperate.

Voices sounded outside.

Alarm surged through her. In midshift, she stopped, furiously trying to change back into her human form. If anyone saw her like this...

Finally, her hands regained their human form. Megan glanced at the mirror. She was normal again.

She yanked open the door and tore into the parking lot. Near a kiosk with brochures and a map of Florida tacked to a bulletin board, a stranger talked with the girls. He wore the gas station logo on his white shirt and he had a spike used for picking up trash. Just an attendant. But his scent was powerful and she knew he was Draicon, not human. He smiled as she approached.

"Nice to see some of us around. Too many mortals around these parts. Y'all visiting or live around these parts?"

"Visiting," she said, glancing at the van.

"The mate and I can show you the good places to hunt, and best places for hanging with our types. Free of pesky mortals."

The twins stared at him with open curiosity. They'd never encountered a friendly Draicon. Her heart thudded hard. Gabriel was replacing the gas nozzle when Jenny tapped on the map.

"Is that where Or-lando is and this Mickey Mouse you told us about? We've never been to Disney's world."

"I don't like mice," Jillian said with a worried look.

"Mickey isn't a real mouse. He's just a play mouse, a cartoon character. Your daddy prob-ably knows all about them," the attendant as-sured them, pointing to Gabriel.

"Oh, he's not our daddy. But Gabriel is nice. He wouldn't turn us in 'cause he only pretends to be bad, like Mickey isn't a real mouse." Jenny beamed.

Panic flowered bright red inside Megan. She smiled at the attendant, who began to back away. "Lily," she said, using the fake name they'd agreed upon, "you know you're not sup-posed to repeat those silly stories your big sister likes to tell you."

The attendant glanced at Gabriel. "That's the legendary Gabriel Robichaux. I've heard of him before. My kind of man, he brings in Shadows after giving 'em a good dose of justice. I heard he slaughtered ten Shadows last year. Beat 'em to death."

Jenny frowned. "Gabriel would never hurt Shadows. He told us that he likes us, and he even fed us hamburgers. He's going to get us to safety."

Astonished shock flared on the man's face right before he whipped out his cell phone, punched in a number. Megan's heart plummeted to her stomach. Gabriel's cover was blown.

Dodging, she barely missed the blow with the stick aimed directly at her. Megan resisted the impulse to fight back. Instead, she herded the girls toward the car, knowing they had little time before real Draicon Enforcers showed up.

They were running again. Always on the run, always from those who hated them and would never let them alone. When would it ever stop?

The Draicon pursued, swinging the stick like a baseball bat. "Get out, get off my property, you freaks!"

Gabriel whirled. His eyes glowed amber, then

flashed red. He growled and lunged for the attendant.

Gabriel tossed him into the air and the man slammed against the wall. Fists clenched, her mate stalked forward.

"You try hurting her, I'll tear you to pieces," Gabriel snarled.

"Let's go. He already called the Enforcers." Megan pulled at his arm.

As she and the twins climbed into the van, Gabriel waved a hand before the attendant, eradicated his memories.

But the call had already been made.

Too late.

Speeding north on Interstate 75, Gabriel opened up all his senses to perceive danger. He stole glances at Megan.

"It's nothing. He didn't hurt me. I'll be fine."

"Look at me, Megan," Gabriel ordered.

Moisture swam in her big blue eyes. He bit back a rich curse. "I could kill him for hurting you."

"He's not the only one. He just did what every other Draicon wants to do."

Disturbing images emerged as he touched his mind to hers. Men leering at her with lust in their eyes, grabbing at her body and thinking they could molest her because she had no rights. Draicon females mocking her ugly dark purple tunic and pants when she longed to wear brightly colored dresses like they did. Even Draicon children jeering and chasing her away from their campfire on the beach.

"I hate how they make me feel," she said in a low voice.

Taking a deep breath, he forced the raging wolf down. "Listen to me, *chère*. Don't give him that power over you. You're better than he is, always will be better than those who strike out just because you're different. Understand?"

A wobbly smile touched her mouth. "One day, my people will be free. I'll see to it, Gabriel. I'll fight for their freedom so the girls won't ever have to be shamed like that again."

He reached over, touched her cheek in a reassuring gesture. Soft silk beneath his fingertips. He withdrew his hand as the beast growled to the surface, aroused now by desire.

Silence fell in the car for a few minutes, interrupted by Jillian's quivering voice.

"Why do they hate us so much, Megan? We never would have hurt him, but they always want to hurt us."

"I don't know, honey. I honestly don't know."

Anger burned through him as he caught sight of the frightened twins.

"I just wanted to know where Disney's World was. Was that wrong? Maybe Mickey doesn't like Shadows, either." Jenny seemed on the verge of crying.

"I bet Mickey does," he assured her.

Gabriel's chest felt hollow. It wasn't Jenny's fault, but his. He should have ensured he and Megan were alone when he had revealed his real identity. He'd been open and honest and now look at them. Their lives at risk because he'd been careless.

Just like he'd been with Simone and Amelia.

Now he stood to lose two more innocents and Megan for the same reason.

Not on my damn watch, he thought in sudden rage.

"If you see anything suspicious, let me know,"

he told her, glancing at the green sign in the distance.

"What about the car? He has a description."

"I cloaked it with my magick." Gabriel gestured to the side mirror. "Look outside."

Instead of a white minivan, their vehicle appeared as a gleaming black Mercedes. Megan glanced at him with respect.

"Are we being followed?" she asked.

"We will be. Every Enforcer south of Canada will be chasing us now."

"Because of the bounty on our heads?"

"Because of the bounty on mine. You and the twins would bring in only six figures. An Enforcer who turns traitor is worth three times that amount." His jaw tightened. "And then they get to watch the show."

"The show…oh God!"

He yanked a blind over the sudden mental image of the council's warden with the castration instrument in his hands. "Sorry," he said. "I'm not used to someone being inside my head yet."

His reassuring smile didn't ease the strain on her paling face. "Don't worry, darling, I've got a cast iron hide too tough for any of them, and I'm fast. If they ever did catch me, I'd trade them my recipe for Magma Sauce for my jewels. Fair trade, I'd say."

"How can you joke about something so serious?" she whispered.

His guts clenched as he shuttered his mind. *Because I can't afford to let you inside me, and see what I'm really feeling.* "I never joke about trading my recipes," he said mildly.

From the backseat, Jenny spoke in a small voice. "Gabriel, Megan, I'm sorry. I'm sorry I told that man. I didn't mean to, it just came out. I didn't mean to get us in trouble."

In the rearview mirror he saw Jillian hug her sister. Both twins looked ashen, tears shimmering in their blue eyes.

He eased the van onto the shoulder, put it into Park. The jocularity was gone. These were children, needing massive reassurance. Their lives had turned around in the space of a few days, they were hunted like animals and now they depended on him. His guts twisted. But he had to soothe their fears.

"Listen Jenny. It wasn't your fault. Understand? Some Draicon get scared of Shadows because they don't understand, or they're afraid of what they can do. They'll use what you tell them against you, but it is not your fault."

"Just like it wasn't your fault when Amelia got hurt?" Jillian whispered.

Clenching his fists, he stared at her. Finally he muttered, "Not the same."

"There are people out there who don't like you, Jilly and Jenny. They want to see you gone because you're different. Even Draicon, with all the powers and shape-shifting, fear what's different, what they don't understand and can't control. Sometimes telling the truth isn't a good idea because they can use your honesty against you."

"Then it's okay to lie?" Jillian asked.

Megan sucked in a breath.

"Not exactly." He chose his words with care. "It means not telling the full truth to people you don't know, like that man back at the gas station. You know how when you first met me, you didn't know me and thought I'd hurt you? You didn't tell me much of anything, did you?"

Jillian looked thoughtful. "Megan doesn't like

to lie and hates us to lie, too. But she did dye our hair so we could hide from people. I guess that's the same as hiding."

"Hiding only until we reach a safe place," Megan interjected.

"Which is necessary when lives are at stake," he countered.

"Yes," she agreed. "But between people who are supposed to be close, there should be only honesty. No secrets. Aren't you the same with your family?"

Gabriel narrowed his gaze. "My family is my own business."

"And so is mine. The twins are my family and they need to know the truth about us, Gabriel."

Shock filled him as she told the girls Gabriel was her destined mate. He wanted to hit his head against the steering wheel.

Was that necessary? he asked her mentally.

I told you, honesty is best with those close to me. I won't keep this a secret from them.

The twins looked delighted, then confused as he grunted and pulled back onto the road. He read the tension radiating in the van. Destined mates, but not happy about it.

Wasn't he a great role model?

To ease the friction, he broke into a Cajun song, coaxing the twins to sing along. When he finished, Megan angled him a curious look.

"Sissy told me a little about Cajun Draicon. They were like us, forced to leave their homes in the north because they were driven out. My family was originally from Maine, but we moved to Shadow Island when I was very young because other Draicon made things difficult for my parents."

He glanced at the mirror to see if anyone was following. Not yet.

"How old are you?" she asked.

"Over a hundred."

"You're very experienced at shifting. I only shifted a few times into a wolf. It seems to come easily to you, like that day at the dock. How do you manage?"

He answered with a grunt.

Megan put her hand on his arm. He tensed at the softness of her palm, the temptation to cave into the wolf's howling lust to possess her in the flesh.

"Sometimes I wish I could blend in better,

like a Normal. Like you do. Maybe then they wouldn't hunt me like I'm an animal. What kind of life is it for the girls? When every one of the Draicon race seems to hate them just for being Shadow? I don't want them to learn to hate back, Gabriel."

"I know," he quietly agreed. "Don't fret yourself, *chère*. They will not be outcast any longer. I'll set them up with a family who loves little ones, no matter where they come from."

"They've been through too much. They need stability and guidance."

"They need love and acceptance more, not treated like animals and caged just because they're different." His fingers gripped the wheel.

Megan stole a glance at him. "You sound as if you're talking about yourself."

He shrugged. "I come from a good family. Long line of proud Cajuns. My granny taught me to cook good food and my Paw Paw, my grandfather, taught me to play the fiddle. My family is close to me."

Even if they are afraid of me sometimes...

"I want the same for the girls. I have to believe someone will want them, even if they are Shadow."

Gabriel tilted down his hat on his brow, caught sight of the backseat. Jillian hugged her sister for comfort. The girls seemed so young and fragile, just like Amelia.

And he had to get them to a safe place before they got caught.

As he pulled into the next lane, he caught a fleeting thought from Megan. It clenched his guts.

What secret from your past are you hiding, Gabriel? Can you ever trust me to tell me what's really going on?

Chapter 8

Even though her insides quivered, Megan resolved to put on a brave front.

Gabriel had doubled back on their trail and now they headed north on the Florida Turnpike. But he said little about their destination.

He'd been terse since pulling off the road. She felt the cold distance grow between them, as if he desired acres of space inside the car's tight confines.

How could he expect them to be lovers if she knew nothing about him? He was reluctant to even tell her his age.

"One hundred ninety-one," he said.

Megan shot him an accusing look. "You were prowling in my mind again."

He shook his head. "No, darling, your question about my age was so loud, it was like a shout in *my* mind. Had I known you had a hang up about my age, I'd have told you sooner." A slow, sexy wink. "How do you feel about older men?"

She smiled, glad he broke the ice. Draicon wolves aged very slowly. Gabriel was in his twenties by human standards. "As long as they're under 900, I'm fine." She studied his long, leanly muscled body, wondering how many women he'd slept with.

"None quite as young as you," he said, smiling at the telltale flush spreading over her cheeks. "I once liked older women."

"How old were you when you lost..." Her voice dropped. "You know, your first."

"Nineteen."

"So young. And she was older?"

He fell silent a moment, then said, "She was ninety-five."

Judging from his darkened expression, it was not a fond memory. "That makes her a cougar, not a wolf."

A low chuckle sounded from beneath the tilted hat. "Were you in love with her?"

A brief nod. Megan pressed on.

"What happened?"

She caught a flash of thought. *Tamara saw my dark side.*

Then he took back his hat, settled it squarely atop his head and tilted down the brim. Megan glanced out the window at the image of their car. Gabriel seemed to expel no energy holding up the illusion. His magick was powerful.

And dark, he'd hinted. She had no more answers than she'd had before.

Why did Gabriel insist he'd killed Amelia? What had he done?

An hour later, Megan drifted into a doze as the twins chattered, absorbed in their game of reading weathered billboards on Florida's Turnpike.

"Look, Gabriel! Disney! Mickey Mouse," Jennifer pointed.

"Sorry, darling, maybe next time," he told her. "Right now we have to get you to a safe house."

"Is this a magick car that will fly us there?" Jillian asked.

If only, he thought. He accelerated and rubbed his right temple with his knuckles. A minute ago, he'd tried contacting Martin. Still no answer, but this time the answering machine picked up with a message stating Martin was away on a business trip and would return in two weeks.

Gabriel had hung up. Martin seldom made business trips.

Still, it was plausible. Martin's was not a safe house, but a backup known only to Gabriel. When something went wrong, the escaped Shadows went to Martin.

Maybe he should leave them with Martin until he could find them safe passage. Every instinct urged him to stick close to their side. Yet how could he guarantee their safety? Their welfare came before all else.

His didn't matter as much. He'd be willing to take risks alone, but not with them.

Beside him, Megan whimpered in her sleep. Gabriel touched her arm. She awoke with a small cry that twisted his heart.

"You were having a nightmare, darling. Bad one?"

She rubbed her eyes. "The same I've had for years. It's nothing."

"Tell me," he urged.

"It's nothing."

Gabriel felt a small disappointment when she closed herself off. Maybe she was still too afraid. "You're safe with me," he assured her in a quiet voice.

Megan gave him a sweet smile. "Thanks for not invading my mind and waking me up the old-fashioned way."

Her honest gratitude lowered the defenses he used to shield himself against the world. Alarmed, he hid behind a cocky grin. "The old-fashioned way would be either through sex or an alarm clock."

Heat suffused her cheeks, making them a delicate pink. Megan looked deliciously sexy, the blue of her eyes soft and welcoming. His gaze slid downward to her lips. A mouth sultry and lush enough to tempt a eunuch.

Which is what he'd become if the council discovered his true nature. The council didn't want to strip his gene pool for helping escapees. No one ever trusted his kind around women. He was far too lethal.

Megan tucked her feet beneath her. The move only made him think of how limber she was, and how flexible she'd be with those long, supple legs wrapped about his waist....

"Can we take a break and get out?" she asked.

He headed for the next exit. Gabriel turned down a country road. He parked the car, and he and Megan got out. She turned her sun-kissed face upward like a flower seeking warmth. Life sparkled in her blue eyes.

"I want to shift into my wolf form."

Her abrupt confession startled him. "It's too dangerous to shift here."

"There's no one around."

"There could be. It's too risky here, Megan. Why the sudden urge?"

She bit the sweet, tempting curve of her bottom lip. "It's been a long, long time and I'm not sure I remember how to become a wolf. I have this crazy need to run as one, to be free and unrestricted. Be free to be myself instead of having to conform to rules and regulations slapped on my people to keep us in place. Too long I've lived in a cage of restrictions. You couldn't understand that."

Gabriel swallowed hard. She was adventurous and brave, and comfortable in her own skin. His skin, wolf or otherwise, felt stretched tight over bone.

"I understand more than you think. I know all about cages and restrictions. When we get to our destination, there's a big backyard where you can shape-shift. Shifting will come back to you."

"Are you sure?"

"You can run free and wild and never stop."

She stretched her arms and the move shifted her shirt upward. He caught a glimpse of pale, creamy flesh on her belly. Suddenly he wanted her hot and naked beneath him. With considerable effort, Gabriel suppressed the beast that demanded he exercise his masculine rights as a bonded Draicon.

"Why are you looking at me like that? What are you thinking about?"

He glanced into the backseat. The twins had stopped watching the movie and were dozing off. "You. What I want to do with you," he said softly.

A pink flush ignited her cheeks. "What do you want, Gabriel?"

Gabriel touched her cheek. Thought about how she'd look beneath him as he took her, her lovely blue eyes dazed with passion, her soft curves pressed against his hard body.

"Right now all I can think about is getting you naked."

Megan moistened her lips as a pulse beat wildly at the base of her throat. His body tightened as he stared at her wet, delectable mouth.

"H-here?" Her melodious voice dropped to a sultry whisper. "What would you do?"

He could scent her arousal and it inflamed his own. "I'd put my mouth between your legs. I can't wait to have the taste of you beneath my tongue. I'd make you beg me to stop, *chère*. Beg me because you couldn't handle it anymore."

This was dangerous, this little fantasy. It invoked an image of her spreading out her arms in welcome for him and watching the dazed pleasure on her face as he brought her to orgasm.

"Oh!"

"I'd take it real slow, and gentle, and let you know what passion is. Kisses all over your sweet skin, marking every inch of you so you'll know you are mine and you'll never forget your first time. Then…when I was sure you were ready, I'd…"

His voice trailed off. Gabriel bit back a moan as she unbuttoned his shirt and slid her palm over his bare skin. The feel of her hand across the thick muscles of his chest made his body clench.

She snatched off his hat and hooked her hands through his thick hair as he pulled her into his arms. Warmth spread through him as he kissed her deeply, her mouth parting as she returned his passion. His tongue stroked long and deep, letting her know what lay ahead, mimicking how his body would thrust into hers.

When they broke apart, her cheeks flushed and her eyes darkened with need. He ran a thumb tenderly over her jaw.

"We need to get going, darling. As much as I want to stay here, and finish this."

"Can't we stay here? It feels safe and no one's following us."

He smiled in understanding, smoothing back her hair. Megan's mouth was pouty and swollen from his hungry kiss. "Not now, *chère*. It's too risky. When the time is right, I'll make you mine."

If only he dared trust her, she wouldn't race away screaming once she knew all his secrets.

Chapter 9

The deep-seated desire between them didn't mean more openness on Gabriel's part. She couldn't even get him to tell her the full truth about where they were going.

The GPS device chimed their location. Megan turned her attention from the electronic map and gave him an accusing look.

"You said we were headed to Orlando. Why are we going west toward Tampa?"

He inclined his head at the still-sleeping girls. "We were headed to Orlando. That's the truth. I didn't want the twins to know our exact location. Just in case they told someone by accident like they did at the gas station. Safer that way."

"I get it. Now can you tell me where we're going?"

He pressed a button on the GPS. "A little town called Burnside. Martin's new safe house is there. Not far from the Orlando safe house."

"New house?"

"I move him around as needed. Less chance of someone fishing out the location."

"I thought there was only one refuge in Central Florida," she told him.

"No one knows about Martin except me. It's a refuge of last resort." His jaw tightened. "The Orlando house may have been compromised."

"How? I thought the network was foolproof. Who would have betrayed us?"

"It's not necessary for you to know."

"And what if something happens and we're stuck or you can't help us?"

A low growl rumbled from his throat. "Are you saying I can't do my job?"

"No, I'm saying I need to know what I'm getting into. This is a little scary for me, running into the unknown. What's going on?"

Gabriel tilted the hat down. "I have no proof, but something's gone bad, I can sense it. The

Friend who was to escort you from Naples to Orlando never showed up and his cell goes unanswered. No one answers at the Orlando house, either. So I'm taking you to Martin's. Last resort to keep you and the girls protected, while I find out what the hell is going on."

A heavy weight settled on her chest. She'd thought they'd be okay before the gas station fiasco. Now she knew they'd been endangered all along. Gabriel took enormous risks to protect them.

"Why didn't you say so before?"

"Natural caution. Compromising my own safety is one thing. But I'll be damned if I risk anyone under my care."

"Thank you," she said, touched by his loyalty. "Why are you doing this for Shadows?"

Pain flashed in his dark eyes. "I used to do it because it *was* risky. For the kicks, the thrills and adventure. No one should be discriminated against just because they're different. My Paw Paw taught me that."

"*Now* why do you do it?"

For a minute, she thought he would not answer. "Because of what happened to Amelia."

He looked away.

"She must have been so special to you. I can't imagine your pain. But I can let you know I'm here for you, if you need me."

The thought flickered like a neon light struggling to stay lit. *I can't have need of you, or anyone. You wouldn't understand how it is.*

"If you let me try, I could," she told him.

Using their unique telepathic connection, she touched her mind to his. Searching for clues, like groping for a light switch in a dark room: a laughing girl with blond hair, riding on Gabriel's shoulders at a Mardi Gras parade. Gabriel polishing the chrome on a sleek new Harley. A beautiful woman reaching out to him in affection...then backing away in horror...

A steel shutter slammed down. Megan winced and rubbed the spike of pain in her head.

"Sorry. But stay out of my mind. You wouldn't like seeing what's inside of me," he said darkly.

If she pushed her right as his destined mate, he'd shut her out even more. "I didn't mean to pry," she began.

At his level look, she admitted. "Okay, I did. What can I say? It's a female thing."

A low chuckle rumbled from his deep chest. Encouraged, she took a chance. "We're mates, Gabriel, and I want to know you better. I've been on my own so long, surviving on instinct, moving from place to place to stay alive. My life has been a minefield, and each step could blow up in my face. This is hard for me, putting our lives in your hands."

"I told you, I won't hurt you or the twins. You need to learn to trust me on this."

"I will, if you learn to trust me, as well."

Tension tightened his chiseled jaw. Gabriel scowled at the road. "Hang on."

He glanced at the side mirror, then did a sudden U-turn. The abrupt move woke the girls and they cried out. While she reassured them, Gabriel made another series of turns that would confuse anyone following them. Finally he guided the car down a dirt road.

It ended before a white cottage with green shutters. Palm trees and sun-dappled oaks ringed the property. The house was remote, but she heard a dog barking in the distance.

"Stay here," he ordered, swinging his long legs out as he opened the door.

Megan watched as he scanned the property. When he told them to follow him, caution returned. Nothing was normal in her crazy world, but something about this place seemed off.

The cottage's concrete steps led to a small, algae-covered porch. A hedge looked sadly lopsided and overgrown, and the grass was brown and patchy.

Gabriel rapped hard five times on the door jamb. A plump, middle-aged woman in a floral dress opened the door.

This was Martin?

"I've come to inquire about the tractor you have for sale. Is it running smoothly?" Gabriel asked.

A sudden gleam sparked the woman's eyes. "It runs as smooth as it must."

She opened the front door wide. "Welcome. All who seek refuge are safe here."

The refuge doesn't look too welcoming, Megan thought as she escorted the girls inside. They sat on a battered leather couch. When the woman went into the kitchen to fetch them something cool to drink, Megan leaned over and whispered to Gabriel.

"Martin is a woman?"

"The code name is Martin. Martin can be any of the retired Friends who no longer help Shadows full-time. They take turns being Martin."

"Who is this then?"

"Angie. I've known her for years. It's okay, *chère*. She's cool."

Megan studied the cheap prints on the yellowed walls, the stained carpet and the thick dust layering the coffee table. Angie wasn't much of a housekeeper. That didn't bother her, but the putrid smell underlying the house did.

"This is all wrong," she said in a low voice as the twins looked around curiously.

Gabriel frowned. "I sense it, as well. But it's part of the cover to keep away intruders. Tell me. You have a gift for using your instinct."

His confidence warmed her. "It's as if you purposely drabbed down the house to make it inconspicuous. But the algae out front, the hedges and this furniture, there's an odor that doesn't belong. New, fresh. It smells like... blood."

Gabriel's nostrils flared. He looked around.

"Angie might have scented the house to ward off strangers. I need to check things out."

"Let me. I'll be less conspicuous. I can turn into Shadow."

Doubt flared on his face. Gabriel rubbed a hand over the dark bristles shadowing his angular jaw. "It's risky."

"I'll be careful."

They fell silent as Angie returned bearing a wooden tray and four tall glasses of iced tea. She sat as they helped themselves.

"I hope y'all are hungry. I just prepared rare meat for you, one of the chickens I keep out back," Angie told them.

It would explain the scent of blood, but she didn't trust the woman's look. Neither did Gabriel, his cowboy hat tilted back as if to better view their hostess.

Gabriel was good, Megan admitted. He engaged Angie in small talk, saying nothing using a lot of words. Angie seemed restless, but responded politely to Gabriel's questions about the weather.

Now. Pretend you're sleepy.

The direct command inside her mind startled

her a moment. Megan covered her mouth as she yawned widely. Gabriel glanced at her. "Angie, mind if she takes a short nap? It's been a long drive."

Angie showed her to a back bedroom. The same musty smell pervaded here. Megan thanked her, and Angie scurried back to the living room.

"Where did y'all start out your journey?" she heard Angie ask.

"South," Gabriel said.

She slipped into Shadow and stepped into the hallway.

The small kitchen was neat and tidy. No scent of fresh blood. Angie lied about killing a chicken. Still invisible, she quietly opened the back door and went outside.

As she reached the forest, the stench of spilled blood thickened the air.

She stubbed her toe on something and looked down. Protruding from the undergrowth was the tip of something round and blue. She touched it.

A woman's leather shoe.

Her heart pounded as she swept aside dead

leaves and pine needles. The body had been hastily buried. Swallowing revulsion, she scraped at earth and leaves until her fingers struck flesh.

The round, plump face of a middle-aged woman stared sightlessly, her mouth frozen in horrified shock. She'd been strangled.

Megan sat back on her haunches, her body shaking. Cold dread pitted in her stomach. This was the real Angie.

That thing back in the living room, alone now with Gabriel and the twins, what was it?

I found a body out back. It's the real Angie. Get the girls out now.

Racing toward the house, her breath violent sobs, she sent the message over and over, hoping it wasn't too late.

Slamming down his anger and worry, Gabriel opened all his Draicon senses. The cold stench of rotting garbage leaked through this Angie's scent. Flatness showed in her hard gaze.

He glanced at the girls, wondering how the hell to get them out without endangering them. If he used his powers…

Jennifer stared at the woman. "What's wrong with your eyes?"

Gabriel suppressed a groan. The guilelessness of the young.

Angie gave a motherly smile. Then she showed all her teeth.

Her yellowed, pointed teeth.

The face shifted to a shade of mottled gray. "I've been waiting for you," grated the cold, dead voice.

Jillian and Jennifer screamed. Megan spoke into his mind. *Get the girls out now.*

Bounding off the sofa, Gabriel scooped up a twin in each arm. "Dammit," he exploded. "It's a setup. Get out!"

As he dumped them outside the porch, the twins ran for the van, their hands fumbling at the door handle.

Who was the plant? Who had betrayed him?

His heart dropped to his stomach as he heard the familiar click of a weapon cocked back. He raised his hands to call forth his powers and destroy the entity who was on the front porch.

Megan rounded the corner.

Stay there, I'm coming for you. Don't move, he ordered.

Shadow replaced Megan's form. Tracking her scent, he sensed her dancing from tree to tree. Gabriel thrust all his powers into the Morph, but the creature resisted his efforts. The Morph raised the gun. Bullets popped and splintered the ground. Gabriel cursed and ran towards Megan as she stepped behind a tree, her form flickering. He pushed her aside and dove forward in the line of fire. The smell of cordite filled the air. A bullet tore through his lower torso. Two more hit his side.

He put a hand to his belly, agony exploding through his side, warmth spreading through his parted fingers. A groan rumbled deep in his chest. He'd survive.

He saw the fake Angie point the weapon toward him. Suddenly, it jerked out of her hands. She gave a loud shriek as it danced in the air.

Jennifer.

Pain and rage roared, bringing out the beast. Gabriel held his stomach, fighting down the instinct to shift and fight. He had to look after Megan and the twins.

Instead he hurled all his magick at the fake Angie, barreling into her head with the force of a tractor trailer. *You have a brain aneurysm rupturing. Your head is exploding in pain. You will die.*

A shrill scream came from near the house. He dragged himself to the van, knowing what would happen. In minutes, the fake Angie would be dead from the power of suggestion.

He crawled into the van as Megan scrambled into the driver's side. She cranked the ignition and hit the gas pedal.

A white-hot razor sliced through his belly. Gabriel bit back a rich curse as he peeled off his shirt. He glanced downward at the blood pumping through his splayed fingers.

Mixed in with the crimson of his life's blood was a sluggish silver liquid.

Megan looked in horror at his wound. "Silver bullets?"

"Worse." He struggled to speak through the pain. "Hollow bullets…liquid silver."

The surest and most painful way to kill him. He slumped on the seat, his guts on fire.

"How bad is it?" Megan gunned the engine.

"Bad enough." He lifted his wet hand. Blood gushed from the wound.

"We have to get you to a hospital." She shot through a stop sign.

"Too dangerous. Be okay. Can't let them get to you."

Then he quieted, because it hurt too much to talk, and he needed to reserve the last of his precious energy. Because he'd be damned if he'd die now that the last safe place had been compromised, leaving Megan and the twins on their own.

Chapter 10

Gabriel was losing a lot of blood. If she didn't do something, he'd bleed out.

Megan glanced in the rearview mirror at her frightened nieces. "Jennifer," she said, knowing the older twin was more able to cope with the emergency, "can you scoot up here by me and help? Take Gabriel's shirt, fold it and press it against his tummy. I need you to stop the bleeding."

Paling gooseflesh springing over her thin arms, Jennifer did as she was asked. His eyes closed, Gabriel tossed his head, groaning. Her cousin was on the verge of crying, but bravely bit her lip to hold back the tears as she pressed against his wound. The blood flow slowed.

Dusk began to drape the blue sky. Megan studied the GPS to figure out where they were going. "Jillian, do you sense anything?"

At her cousin's head shake, she made a decision. As they approached a small, narrow road bordering a field, she studied the abandoned barn sitting by the fence.

"Hang on."

She pumped the brakes to not leave a rubber trail, and made an abrupt left turn onto the dirt road.

Some distance away from the main road, she parked the van beneath a copse of trees. Hidden from view by thick scrub, it would suffice.

She lifted an unconscious Gabriel, using her wolf strength to carry him as gently as possible.

Ever self-sufficient, Jennifer and Jillian gathered leaves and branches to form a makeshift lean-to shelter. Her heart ached as she remembered when they'd done the same on Shadow Island, after being evicted because a Draicon liked her grandmother's beachfront house.

Beneath the sprawling branches of a live oak, she laid Gabriel down. Megan put a pillow she'd found in the minivan beneath his head.

She fetched a blanket and tucked it around him, checking on his wound.

Overhead against the leaden skies, a red hawk circled as if sensing wounded prey below. She glanced upward, splaying her arms protectively over her mate. Megan stroked his brow, knowing how much pain he suffered. He woke up, writhing and moaning.

"Quiet," she soothed. "You have to stay still, let Jenny get the bullet out."

Gabriel stilled. Megan opened the first aid kit he'd packed and fished out a small box from her backpack. Contained inside were herbs she used for emergencies and a few steel instruments.

Sweat poured down Gabriel's face as he grit his teeth. Alarmed at the paleness of his tanned skin, which indicated shock, she turned him on his side. Two bullets had exited. The third in his stomach was lodged there.

She sterilized the probe and sank it into the wound as Gabriel breathed through his clenched teeth. Finally, she set down the probe and turned to Jenny.

"It's in two pieces. Remember how Gram

taught you, Jenny? See the pieces in your mind and call them to you."

Using her telekinetic powers, Jennifer began extracting the bullet pieces. Gabriel's dark eyes flashed amber, then red.

Jennifer pulled out a bullet fragment, but his fingers dug into the ground and he growled. Backing away, Jennifer's eyes grew wide. "I can't do it, Megan. I'm scared."

"I'm scared, too, honey, and so is Gabriel."

But she wasn't a dangerous wolf. His wolf might take over and instinctively lash out at anyone, even an innocent girl trying to help him.

"Keep working, Jenny, and let me try something."

Her mouth trembling, her cousin resumed.

Megan dabbed at the flowing wound and began to softly sing. The lines of strain on his brow evened out.

When Jenny finished, small pieces of metal lay on the ground, coated with Gabriel's flesh and blood.

"Now the hard part, honey. You have to get the liquid silver out."

"I can't, Megan, I just can't do it!"

"Think of it like a game, Jenny. You play it by finding every little bit of silver, calling it out and you win when each drop is removed."

Jennifer did as Megan instructed. She gave a triumphant smile when the last droplet was removed and flew into the cup Jillian held out.

Megan wiped Gabriel's body with soft gauze. She applied the liniment, watching the wounds close as she did. The worst was over but for the pain. It would take a while for his body to mitigate the effects of the silver that had been in his system. The next eight hours would be dicey and painful for him.

She used the last cold bottle of water to wet a cloth. Megan stroked his brow, crooning to him as his big body tensed. His jaw ground violently. Suddenly his eyes snapped open. Amber eyes flashing red. In his pain his wolf emerged.

"Hold on, Gabriel, I'm here. I'm not leaving you. I'm here. Can you feel my hand? You can get through this. Just concentrate on me."

Singing might keep the wolf at bay. Megan began a song in the Old Language she'd learned from her grandmother, about where the Draicon first lived, a land of lush green fields and forests, where the sky was blue and the sea waters green.

When his jagged breaths eased and his chest moved evenly up and down, she knew he finally slept. She gently pulled her hand away and pressed a kiss to his forehead.

The twins looked anxiously at her as darkness fell. In the night, they could see well, but it didn't prohibit childish fears.

The van was equipped with emergency supplies, including a small gas lantern and matches. She enlisted their help to set up camp with the lantern, and broke out the remaining room temperature water and the sandwiches Gabriel had purchased at the gas station. After they ate, Megan tucked the girls into a makeshift bed. She covered them with clothes from their suitcases. They turned to wrap their arms around each other as if still in the womb.

Clasping her arms around her bent knees, she watched over her little group, waiting for dawn to break. When Gabriel woke up again, she sang to calm him.

She remained at his side through the night.

* * *

When he opened his eyes, streaks of pink and purple stroked over the dawning sky. Gabriel struggled to sit up. The pain was gone, but damn, he was weak as a pup.

Megan slept by his side, her arms wrapped around the girls. His heart turned over at her sweet, innocent expression.

He needed to find them a place to lie low while he regained his strength and found out what the hell was going on.

Gabriel slipped from beneath the blanket.

Megan and the girls slept on.

He looked at her, his mate, the one he would mark for his own, a female of great courage and strength. Thought of how she'd suffered, the indignities and the injustices and the hurts. Gabriel tilted back his head to release a roaring shout.

It came out as a low, mournful howl.

Giving one last glance at the sleeping trio, he ran off into the woods.

Gabriel was gone.

Using water from a small creek, the twins

had washed up. Megan bathed and washed her hair. The black dye ran out, leaving the strands their natural honey blond. The twins sat quietly. Hunger pinched their faces. The stale gas station store sandwiches had done little last night to ease their rumbling bellies.

They needed to find food.

A soft rustling in the undergrowth sent her heart racing. A branch snapped as a large gray wolf entered their small compound. Its amber eyes glowed with a fierce light, but it approached with hesitation, as if uncertain of welcome.

"It's okay, girls. It's only Gabriel," she told them softly.

Wonder replaced fear as the twins regarded the monster wolf padding toward them. The wolf opened its jaws and dropped a dead rabbit at Megan's feet. He looked up at her expectantly, then trotted off, as if he thought he didn't belong here.

She called softly to him, but the wolf still edged away.

"Gabriel, where are you going?" Jennifer and Jillian called out, as well.

Megan squatted down on her haunches, held out her hand. *I'm here, Gabriel, and I'm not afraid and neither are the twins. Thank you for the rabbit. The girls are so hungry. Have you eaten well? Are you still hurting? Please come back. I'm worried and we need you here with us in case something happens.*

The wolf turned back to her. It was important, she realized. The wolf's first instinct was to protect and defend.

Gabriel loped over to the girls. Jennifer and Jillian rubbed his ears, coaxing out a low, pleasurable whine from the wolf. He sank to his haunches, watching her with amber eyes as she set about preparing the rabbit. After it was spitted and cooking over a small fire, she settled near him, stroking the back of his head.

The wolf watched the girls poke at the fire with long sticks. Even though he clearly enjoyed Megan caressing his gray fur with the pads of her fingers, his eyes did not close and he remained vigilant.

Do you think we can move out by tomorrow?

We must, ma petite chou. *I don't dare risk any more time here. It's too dangerous.*

What about your strength?

The wolf softly growled. *I can handle myself.*

Okay, she'd hit a sensitive nerve. Megan's hand stilled on his soft fur as she remembered what she'd discovered yesterday.

There's something I forgot to tell you. It's important. When I found the real Angie's body...

A gust of anguish swept into her mind, sharp and clear. Megan felt his pain over losing someone close.

I should have insisted she stay in New Orleans when she begged to come help in the Shadow network. Why the hell did I let her? She would still be alive.

The wolf's thoughts, unlike Gabriel in human form, were pure and honest and stark. Megan seized the chance to gain his trust.

I'm sorry, I'm so sorry about what happened to Angie. But it's not your fault, understand? You are not responsible. It was a decision she made and we can't be responsible for other people's decisions.

While caressing behind his ears, she telepathically praised his courage, strength and loyalty. Gradually he relaxed and the icy tide of anguish faded. The wolf finally laid his head between his paws.

Megan, you were saying something about finding Angie's body. What else did you find?

Despite the hot, sultry Florida air, cold dread curdled in her stomach.

The Morph wasn't working alone. I found a few Draicon hairs.

Suddenly alert, the wolf sat up. *Tell me. What color?*

Silver.

Chapter 11

By midafternoon the following day, they were on the move again.

Gabriel had found a cottage to rent by a small lake. The community was quiet, and their closest neighbor was a half-mile away. Best of all, the cabin's perimeter was surrounded by fenced-off woods, even if Megan doubted it would keep away Morphs.

They ditched the van for an abandoned Chevy at a closed gas station. The Chevy belched blue smoke and its engine wheezed. Springs stuck through the torn upholstery and Megan had to shift her bottom to avoid getting poked. Gabriel was concerned the van had a tracking device in it. She felt safer in the Chevy than the van, which was like "waving the scent of fresh meat before a bayou gator," as he put it.

"The van has our scent stamped all over it. I'm not taking chances," he told her.

He'd used a credit card with a fake name to rent the house. Gabriel was like an international spy, she realized. He had more means of identification than the average person. The network for helping Shadows had been well secured. Until now.

Driving west on Highway 60, he turned on a long stretch of two-lane road flanked by pastures and woods. Sugar sand spilled down an embankment.

"We'll stay here only a couple of days, *chère.* I just need a base to work from until I find out how many in the network have been compromised, and where to go from here." He grimaced and held a hand to his side.

"And rest," she urged. "You must rest, Gabriel."

"I will, *ma petite chou.*"

"What does that mean?"

"It's Cajun for 'my little cabbage.'"

At her outraged look, he grinned. "Translated into 'sweetheart.' An endearment."

Shortly before dusk, he pulled into a dirt road flanked by sprawling trees.

While Gabriel prowled the property's perimeter to shield the boundaries against Morphs, the twins explored the house. With their typical efficiency, they had found a room to sleep in, hauled in all the luggage and discovered a bag of cookies in the pantry.

They were sitting at the oaken kitchen table, eating, when she walked in.

"There's only two bedrooms so guess you and Gabriel will have the big one. Jilly and me already claimed the one with the two small beds," Jenny crowed.

Megan turned to hide her telltale flush. "Jilly and I."

"I like Gabriel," Jillian chimed in. "I was so afraid he would die, but when Jenny pulled the bullet out of him, I felt his pain ease. And then you sang, Megan, and it really helped him. He's not dreaming of fire anymore." She reached for a chocolate chip cookie.

Jenny looked solemn. "He needs you, Megan.

I feel it, too. When can we have dinner? I'm hungry."

She kissed the top of her cousin's head. "Me, too, sweetie. Stay here, I'm going to unpack."

The larger bedroom had a king-sized bed covered with a bright blue homespun quilt. A pleasurable shiver skated down her spine as she thought of Gabriel's big body covering hers while they rolled between the sheets. Megan tossed her backpack on the bed and removed the dirty laundry. She found a washing machine and tossed in a load with the girls' soiled clothing, then returned to the bedroom. With some hesitation, she removed the tiny china figurine from her knapsack. It was her most precious item.

The house felt warm and welcoming. The pine chest of drawers was empty. She set the figurine on top.

"Now it looks like home," she whispered. "Will I ever have a real home again?"

Gabriel came in through the kitchen's back door, stomping mud off his boots. "Good property. No scents, except a few animals and boar. Small game adequate for you to hunt later,

Megan. I need a shower and then I'll go into town to get supplies. We'll hole up here for at least three days."

He peeled off his damp shirt.

Her breath sucked in at the magnificent sight of his bare chest. His torso was flat and studded with muscle. A line of hair marched downward, vanishing into the waistband of his faded jeans.

She studied the bullet scars, marveling at how well he'd healed.

When she drew back, sexual heat flared in his eyes. Gabriel ran a finger down her cheek.

"Tomorrow night," he murmured. "By then I'll be at full strength. And then I'll make you mine."

Anticipation shivered through her.

After lunch the following day, Gabriel vanished.

He'd spent the night on the sofa to "avoid temptation," as he had put it. The easy atmosphere had eased them into a relaxed routine. It was possible to imagine they were a family, and this was their cozy cottage.

Looking up from a home and country magazine, she glanced at the window. In the back-yard, the twins played on the swing.

Megan went to find Gabriel.

The front yard was large and grassy and sloped down toward the lake. Gabriel stood at the wooden dock.

She watched him for a moment, a different kind of hunger growing inside her. What would it finally feel like to be in his arms, having him hold her close as they made love?

She shivered as she remembered other males who'd wanted her for another, more sinister reason.

Gabriel glanced over his shoulder and cracked an encouraging smile. "*Chère.* You all right? You look like there's a gator chasing you."

"Better an alligator than what is chasing us." She stood beside him, feeling the sexual tension thicken between them. Megan breathed in his enticing scent of pine and leather and man. "Sometimes I wonder if I can ever stop moving from place to place. It's so unsettling."

"I know." His gaze hardened as he stared at the lake. "I've never lived anywhere longer than three years. Not since I was nineteen. My parents asked me to find my own place. Said it was best for everyone."

The quiet, rare admission touched her. "What about your pack? They're your family, your life's blood."

"They thought it was a good idea, too."

She wanted to ask more, but he tensed. "We need to talk. I've put off telling you this because you needed to rest and so did the girls. I don't know who is chasing us, how they found out the one safe house I've kept secret for so long. That Morph wasn't there by chance. Someone set us up."

"The silver-haired man."

His jaw clenched as he braced his palms on the wood railing. "He's good. Too good. Like a bounty hunter, he's learned to tamp down his scent and use any means at hand to catch and kill his prey."

"What about other safe houses?"

"Too risky. By now the entire network's been compromised. Someone's been leaking information about the locations."

She sucked in a trembling breath. "Why is the silver-haired man chasing us? What does he want? The twins. Or me? I've had trouble before with men…."

Gabriel turned and placed his warm palms on her shoulders. "What kind of trouble, Megan?"

Embarrassed, she could not meet his gaze. He tipped up her chin with one finger. "Hey, you can tell me, darling. You have nothing to be ashamed of."

Megan finally met his gaze. "Men…they've started to steal away female Shadows. For sex. There are Draicon mercenaries kidnapping Shadows for pleasure houses on Shadow Island."

Anger dawned in his dark chocolate eyes. "Forced prostitution."

Words stuck in her throat. She forced them out. "Draicon believe that sex with a female Shadow is the ultimate aphrodisiac. They especially like the untouched, because it's said virgins enhance a male's own magick. It's one reason Gram kept moving us, to try to keep me hidden. Six, maybe eight times in the past year. I lost track. Once, twice, we were homeless and had to sleep on the beach."

The horror of those times sliced into her

mind. Leering faces of the mercenaries chasing them, taunting her with the things they wanted to do. The rain dripping on her neck from the palm trees. Damp cold biting into her grandmother's ancient bones, despite the blankets Megan heaped on her. The brave front of the twins as they ignored the constant grumbling of their empty stomachs.

"The governor is in on the scheme. His staff tattooed me. They said it was to keep track of the Shadows on the island, but only the younger females get them. I'm number 00-44. I found out the ink had a special tracking device so I had Gram…cut it out."

The agonized pain of that crude surgery was still fresh. Men saw her only for her body. They didn't care about her as an individual, how she liked to hunt for shells at low tide, or how seeing photos of the twins' mother made her weepy and reminded her of losing her own parents ten years ago. How her favorite pastime had been teaching the Shadow children about their world, trying to expand their visions and give them hope for a better tomorrow.

Gabriel gave her a tender, searching look.

"Megan, you are much more than what they think of you. You're safe now, and no one will ever force you against your will. Understand?"

He slid a hand around the back of her neck, his strong fingers curling around her nape. Gabriel began a soothing massage. "You're Megan, not a number. You're exceptional and unique and no one can ever take that away from you. Never let them. You have so much more to offer the world."

His thumb stroked over the scarred flesh on her nape, assuaging her fears and painful past. Megan closed her eyes, savoring the heat from Gabriel's gentle touch as it chased away bitterly cold memories.

When he pressed his mouth against hers, touched the corner of her mouth with his, his kiss was a reassurance.

Hot tears stung her eyes. She blinked them away furiously, and turned aside. Being this vulnerable caught her off guard. It was oh so tempting to lean against his strength, let him absorb her pain, but he shared little in return. She wanted more than a man who would hold her when she cried.

She needed one who allowed her to hold him when he cried, as well.

"I ran away to save myself, but the girls are my first priority. I have to get them to New Orleans."

"Why?" The question was stark, demanding.

"I have a sealed letter from my grandmother that I'm supposed to deliver to someone who will help them."

Gabriel's expression grew wary. "The letter may explain why this man is so intent on finding you. He's become a damn Morph to gain more power, he's that desperate or that evil. This kind, I know him. He won't quit until he has what he wants."

A shiver went through her at the dangerous glow in his eyes. Gabriel was equally ruthless. He would not relent, either.

"Who's getting the letter?"

Her hands gripped the wood railing. "Someone you know quite well." It was time to tell him. "Your brother, Alexandre Robichaux. The man who's known to all Shadows as the one who helps them gain new identities."

A frown creased his brow. "I know what Alex

does, it's the system we both set up to aid Shadows. But why would your grandmother write him? All you need are the correct code words and those are always memorized."

"It's a letter to Alexandre asking for a favor. Gram wants him to try to find the twins' real father."

"I don't get it."

A gust of wind skated across the lake. She rubbed her suddenly chilled hands. "The twins have never known their father. They were left on Shadow Island by their mother shortly after she gave birth, and Sissy gave them to our grandmother to raise. She said it was safer for them on the island. This was before the council made it into a prison. Sissy, my cousin, said that the world outside was cold and heartless to Shadows. She'd experienced it even among her mate's family; his parents kept trying to keep her from using her Shadow powers, to fit into their world instead."

"Megan, we need to open that letter. It could be the reason the silver-haired man has followed you."

"Do you think he's the twins' father? He's

trying to kill them so no one knows he fathered Shadows?"

Her racing heart slowed as Gabriel stroked her hair. "No, *chère*. I didn't sense that when I picked up his trail back on my island. It almost seemed like he wasn't even after the girls."

"Me? Could he be another Draicon mercenary?"

"Maybe."

He kissed the top of her head. "You're blond." Amusement threaded through his deep voice. "Guess your disguise washed out."

"So are the girls. They look a little like their mother. This beautiful shade of white-blond that catches the light and tosses it back like diamonds on water."

Gabriel went still. "Not many Draicon or Shadows have that color. I knew someone…"

"What?"

"Later. I'm going to patrol the property. We'll open the letter when they're in bed, in case the news is something that might upset them. Let the girls get into a normal routine, *chère*. They know you best and it will be good for them. These kids have been under too much stress, seen too much. It will be good for you, as well. I don't want them using their powers. The spectral trail they may leave could attract the wrong attention."

"The girls never use their powers without permission. We teach our children when they are young Shadows to curb their impulses, and discipline them when they use their magick without our permission. They're only allowed it to save themselves or others from extreme danger. And the trail they leave is so faint, it takes a lot of power to flush it out."

"If only Draicon knew, maybe they wouldn't fear Shadows as much. They fear what they don't understand. Some day, maybe they will." He curled his hands into tight fists. "This new governor, he's worse than I heard. Females should be revered and protected, not abused."

She gave a sad smile. "If only other Draicon thought as you did. Shadows I knew were captured as sex slaves. I cried when they tattooed me, thinking I'd suffer their fate, too."

"Never." He drew her into his arms. "You're mine, Megan. I always protect my own."

"I'm my own person, Gabriel. I ran away to make my own choices."

"Then I'll have to convince you."

Chapter 12

Silvery moonlight dappled the Spanish moss dripping from the live oak branches. Wind rustled through the trees, stirred the carpet of dead leaves on the moist grass. Her eyes adjusted to the inky night as the woods beckoned her animal side. Megan stared up at the full moon, hoping it would help her transition into wolf.

Anxiety coursed through her. It had been so long, and she yearned to run wild and free. Yet what if she couldn't shift? Something that came as normal and natural to Draicon had been denied her. Shadows had a harder time shifting than Draicon because of their tremendous abilities to cloak themselves. Their DNA was different.

The back door opened and Gabriel stepped out. His long-legged, confident stride sent a tingle down her spine. She watched in sheer sexual interest. Clad in jeans and a button-down blue shirt with the sleeves rolled up to display muscled forearms, he was barefoot.

"I checked on the girls before coming out." Gabriel rubbed a hand over his night whiskers. "They're such cute sweethearts when they're asleep. Their hair is blond now, too. Haven't seen a color like that in a long time," he remarked again. Then he looked her square in the eye. "What are you doing out here?"

She swallowed hard. "I want to run with the moon." Hated having to ask, but he was Draicon. "Will you show me?"

Gabriel said nothing for a moment. Then he gave a brisk nod. "I'll teach you, but I'm not shifting tonight."

"Why?"

"Let's focus on you. Ready to do this, darling?"

The husky whisper in the night caressed her. Megan nodded and swallowed hard.

"Take your clothes off."

She stared at his unsmiling face. "When I shift, my clothes vanish. Why should I get undressed?"

"It'll make the transition easier on your body if your magick doesn't have to take care of the clothes."

He stood in silence, watching her. She wanted this so badly, her hands shook as she stripped. Naked, she lifted her chin and faced him. A shaft of silver moonlight speared through the live oak tree and spilled on her right breast.

Gabriel heaved in a ragged breath. "Now, lift your face to the moon. Remember what it was like. Remember the wolf inside you, the animal longing to be free and run with the wind. You can do it."

Natural authority rang out in his deep voice. She summoned the wild beast, the wolf that had once enjoyed running along the beach, snapping at seagulls on her island home. Megan stretched out her arms in a plaintive plea for her body to cooperate.

Blue and red sparks shimmered in the air. The change was happening! She felt her bones lengthen, fur ripple along her spine.

Then it stopped. She glanced down to see herself still on two legs, her hands normal.

Still human.

She slammed a fist against her thigh. "I can't do it. What's wrong with me? Why can't I be like a Normal? It's so easy for them, I just want to run with the moon!"

"It will happen. Just give it another try. C'mon, darling, you can do it. I know you can."

Taking a deep breath, she tried once more. This time, no sparks filled the air, as if her magick had well and truly died.

"Your body may need more protein, more energy. You've been under a lot of stress, Megan."

Excuses, she thought, her stomach twisting in knots. He was trying to make her feel better.

Nothing could make her feel better, not when she was denied something she wanted so very much. How could she ever blend if she couldn't even shape-shift?

"I have to be alone for a while."

Picking up her clothes, she ran toward the lake. On the slope of the front lawn, she threw her clothing down and sat on it. Megan hugged her knees, staring at the water.

What was wrong with her?

"Nothing's wrong with you. It'll just take time, that's all."

She heard the thwack of a blanket snapping out but ignored him as he sat down beside her. Gabriel patted a spot. "C'mere, *chère*. I won't bite and the blanket is softer than your clothing."

No reply. He couldn't understand what she was going through, how freakish she felt for her defect. The one thing that connected her with Normals, the one ability she had that would enable her to blend into this world, was gone.

"I have no future, no hope," she finally whispered.

"Quel espoir et quel avenir, mais, moi, je vais avoir?"

She turned her head toward him.

"What hope and what future am I going to have? I've often thought that before. Tell me what you are going through. I want to help."

"You wouldn't understand."

"I might, more than you think," he said darkly. "Talk to me."

Finally she joined him on the blanket. Megan stared at the water, emotion clogging her throat. "When I was younger, after the time when all Draicon go through the Change, the Draicon teens visiting our island used to tease me because I couldn't run with them. I'd try and try to shift, but by the time I became wolf, they were long gone, running down the beach."

Tears finally trickled down her cheeks. "And now, when I need it most, not because some kids are mocking me, but because I have to blend into this world and pretend I'm normal to be accepted, I can't do it. I feel so alone."

Cupping her face in his palms, he turned her toward him. Moonlight splashed over his angular features, reflected in the gentleness in his dark eyes. Gabriel wiped away her tears with a thumb. "Megan, I know all about being different, and hiding what you really are. You are not alone. Shifting into a wolf is part of what we are, but it isn't who we are. That's inside, in here."

He touched her bare chest. "Only you can

decide that. Who Megan is, the qualities that you have, your spirit and your fire. They can never take that away from you. And if you must hide some of the things that others won't accept or understand, remember that spirit inside you that will always burn bright."

"But I don't want to hide, Gabriel." Megan put her hands on his wrists, anchoring him, needing his understanding as well as his strength. "I want to be free, open, and accepted for who I am."

"Sometimes that's not possible. People won't accept you, no matter how hard you try to get them to understand your true nature holds no harm for them."

Insight filled her. "What is your true nature, Gabriel? What are you hiding?"

She would ask that question. Gabriel's jaw worked hard as he dropped his hands. For a long moment he said nothing. Finally he settled on a truth.

"My true nature is that of a bonded male for his female."

A quivering breath, and a soft touch upon

his arm. So silky. His brain blanked out at her sweet, still-innocent scent. Fresh wildflowers sprinkled with feminine musk.

Raw sexual need roared as his gaze swept over her supple, naked body. The curve of her hips, her slender waist, the lush bounty of her breasts…

Beneath his jeans, his cock hardened at the thought of laying her back and tasting all that sweet flesh beneath his tongue.

His animal sensed she wouldn't be in heat for a week yet, so sex was safe. No chance of making babies who would turn out like him.

Male possessiveness filled him. The animal inside wanted nothing between them but skin. A snarl rose in his throat. He choked it down, not wanting to scare her.

Gabriel gambled on a confession. "I have a tendency when I get emotional…to get Feral."

Anxiety flared in her gaze. He touched her mind, saw her fear of Feral wolves, their savagery, their animal halves often taking over the human side. Gabriel sent her his reassurances. *I will never hurt you.*

He flexed his long fingers. "It happens when

I get sexually aroused by you, as well. I don't want to hurt you, Megan. I'd never hurt you."

"I'm not afraid. Gabriel, look at me."

When his gaze finally met hers, she took his face into her hands. Sugar-spun blond hair tumbled past her slim shoulders. Wide blue eyes the color of a deep, still lake regarded him. Her heart-shaped, exotic face had a delicate air, but Megan was tough as honed steel. He relished her fighting spirit.

The gentleness of her touch made him tremble with yearning. Tenderness wasn't part of his world. His brothers roughhoused, fought alongside him. His parents loved him, but kept their distance. He craved a connection with her, ending the constant loneliness. Everyone in his close circle, even those unaware of his powers, respected and feared him. Past lovers enjoyed his wildness in lovemaking, and were equally fierce in their need, often leaving their nail scratches across his muscled back.

He craved Megan's softness and tenderness.

"Maybe this is why we're meant to be together. Because you know what I do, that in here—" she took his hand and placed it over her heart "—is what we should never hide."

"I don't want to hide from you, Megan." He hissed as the beast clawed in fierce need.

Her voice dropped as she caught the wild look in his eyes. "What's wrong, Gabriel?"

"I don't know if I can control it. The man inside me wants to love you slow and long, *ma petite chou*. The wolf wants to mate."

Her pupils dilated. The scent of her arousal obliterated all sense. Gabriel fisted his hands. Primal instinct took over, his powerful body ready to penetrate, claim and conquer. The beast growled in approval as he envisioned mounting her naked body, letting his mate feel his enormous strength, his virility. Hearing her erotic moans sing in his ear as she arched up to meet him as he sank deep inside her.

He could no longer wait.

Gabriel's eyes flashed amber.

His shirt came off with a powerful rip, buttons exploding from the seams like bullets. "Have to feel you under me," he muttered, tumbling with her to the blanket.

Beneath each stroke of his hands she trembled. Her body sang with life, her breasts heavy and full. Megan strained against him as she wriggled to draw him closer. He caught her breasts in his palms and gently squeezed. Sensations sizzled through her as his thumbs rubbed against her pearling nipples.

"I need your mouth," he growled. Gone was the haunting, musical lilt of his Louisiana accent.

The kiss was demanding, insistent. Savage possession was in each deliberate thrust of his tongue. Wet heat gathered between her thighs. She ached, her body hot and yearning for something she couldn't define.

Then all his guards dropped and she saw into the heart of him. The beast, shaking with desire to touch and claim her as his own. The feel of her soft, naked body beneath his sending him spiraling out of control.

Dark eyes flashing amber. Mine, the wolf snarled. *All mine.*

Breath caught in her lungs as he unbuckled and unzipped his jeans. He pushed them past his thighs. His penis sprang out, reddened and stiff, thick as her wrist.

Dark silky hair spilled over his wide shoulders. Intent glittered in his gaze. His control splintered as he spread her legs wide. Gabriel leaned over her, his stiffened cock stroking against her thigh.

He would take her without thought, without care. The Feral need to mate and claim pushed away her Gabriel, the one who had regarded her tenderly moments ago. Fear and desire warred inside her.

Trembling, Megan reached out for the man she knew.

"Please, Gabriel. Come back to me." In utter trust, she held his gaze as he pinned her wrists to the blanket.

Pushing off her, he hovered, uncertain. Gabriel stared down at her. A heartbeat of silence quivered in the moist night air.

"Touch me, Megan." He took her hand, guided it to his face. "Let me feel your warmth, your gentleness. No one's been like this to me in a long time."

The ache in his deep voice turned her heart

over. Megan cupped his face, soothing away the Feral beast with each slow stroke of her thumbs. Long lashes swept down to his cheeks as he closed his eyes on a shuddering sigh.

Gabriel bent his head and nuzzled her neck. Breathing in her scent. His mouth was warm and firm as he slid a trail of kisses along her throat.

A thought flashed from him over and over. The yearning to please her, to make it special and show her how high passion could take her.

Gone was the beast. He pressed a soft kiss to her mouth, his eyes filled with warm tenderness.

He undressed. Gabriel knelt before her. Hunger rose as she stared at his sleekly muscled flanks, the broad torso sprinkled with dark hair. His limbs were strong and powerful. A hank of dark silk spilled over his forehead.

Megan slid her arms around her wolf, demonstrating her own need. Her kiss spoke of yearnings and dreams. Bonding with her mate, having a place where she at last belonged.

She sensed the beast was leashed as he responded, his kiss a lazy and sensual stroke of his tongue. Heat sizzled between them.

Turning on her side, she moved against him, restless and now impatient. His eyes opened as he gave her a tender look.

"Slow," he whispered against her mouth. "Easy, *chère.* We'll take it slow, make you ready for me."

"I want to be one with you, Gabriel."

His big hands explored. A long, lazy stroke down the arch of her spine. Megan sensed his fierce control, the power inside him tapped, the ferocious, protective Draicon desired now only to pleasure her.

So many hidden layers to her Gabriel. The courageous fighter. The protective, wary Draicon. The duality of roles he played in helping Shadows. He'd suffered tremendous loss, and yet he pushed on, meeting each challenge with determination.

Then he again cupped her breasts and slowly thumbed them, arousing her need. Whetting her own passion. His mouth encased one hard nipple. A haze of passion clouded her mind as he suckled her, his tongue swirling and stroking. Driven by her own feral need, she pumped her hips upward in nameless longing. Gabriel released her nipple. Rolling her onto her back, he smiled tenderly and slid a hand down her hip, delved teasingly into the damp curls.

Stunned, she instinctively slammed her legs shut.

"Open up for me, *chère.* Let me in," he whispered.

His fingers stroked, slid between her soaked folds. Megan clutched his broad shoulders as he touched the aching, shivering flesh. Each caress erased past fears. He slid a finger deep inside her, teased. Fire mounted within her, licking and then roaring into an inferno.

Megan arched and cried out his name as she shattered. When her body finally ceased shuddering, she saw frank male satisfaction gleam in his eyes.

He dropped a gentle kiss on her mouth, rubbed his cheek against hers. Rough bristles abraded her soft skin.

Settling his lean hips between her legs, he looked down at her.

"Look at me," he softly ordered. "I need to see your eyes when I take you."

Jaw tightened, he slowly pushed inside her. The pressure built, stretching and burning. Megan grit her teeth as he slid past her innocence. He felt hard and thick, her inner muscles shuddering to accommodate him. She writhed, trying to find some ease as he penetrated fully. A small tear trickled out of the corner of her eyes. He gently kissed it away.

"Shh," he murmured. "Relax, *ma petite chou.*"

He remained motionless, as if waiting for her. Pain faded slightly. Megan slid her arms up around his neck, feeling the tensile muscles there. Her bonded mate. Her wolf. She moved her hips upward and felt him withdraw slowly, then thrust again.

A hint of untamed danger lurked in his eyes. The Feral beast, barely held at bay. As if to anchor himself more closely to her, Gabriel laced his fingers through hers.

A delicious friction began with each powerful stroke. Gabriel's muscled shoulders flexed as he strained over her. She sensed the beast howling with need, the clawing demand for rough, uninhibited sex. Megan squeezed his fingers.

In silent understanding, she whispered into his mind. *I can take you, Gabriel. All of you. I want all of you.*

He consumed her, filled every pore with awareness of him. For a moment, their spirits tangled together fiercely, the Feral wolf and the emboldened Shadow. Megan lost herself in pure sensation as his silky chest hair rubbed against her tender breasts, his muscular abdomen sliding against her soft belly. She arched to meet his rhythm as the heat between her thighs intensified.

His thrusts came harder and faster and then he stiffened. Megan watched him throw back his head, cords on his powerful neck straining.

With an inhuman cry, he released himself into her. The warmth of his seed spurted deep inside her. He shuddered as the orgasm tore through him and she felt him swell inside her. Something sizzled and raced through her. It felt like a million dancing points of pleasure. She writhed, straining from the erotic sensation.

Murmuring her name, Gabriel collapsed

atop her. His ragged breaths feathered over her cheeks as he buried his face against her neck. She bore his weight, stroking his sweat-dampened hair.

"What was that?" she whispered. "At the end, it felt like…"

"My magick. My powers." He raised himself off her with a solemn look. "When I come inside your body, I fill you with my magick, as well. All our cells contain our powers, so when a male releases inside a female, she receives some of his magick. It's why I never have sex without a condom. Except with you."

He nuzzled her cheek. "Ah, I'm not like other males, also, so when I come…I get bigger. It will take a few moments. If I pull out now, I could hurt you."

Rolling over, he let her sprawl over his body. Wanton and savage need swirled in her. Megan sighed happily, knowing they were bonded in the flesh.

Chapter 13

She was his.

The thought of having her for life made his pulse soar. Gabriel hummed as he put butter into a pan and began frying onions and mushrooms to make omelets. If she didn't like it, he'd make her something else. Warm with sexual possession, he cooked Megan breakfast while the twins slept on.

Every day would be like that with her, and then when the kids came along, lots of kids, he wanted a big family and hoped she did, as well....

Stricken by the thought, Gabriel stopped. Children? With his defect?

A family was as out of reach for him as a star.

Even Megan, with her unique and wonderful abilities as Shadow, didn't have to worry about passing on a defect. Not like him.

Deep grief replaced the honest joy. Gabriel closed his eyes, seeing Amelia's smiling face, her innocent trust. He didn't deserve to have children. Not after how he'd betrayed his sister-in-law and niece.

Hands encircled his waist and softness nestled against his back. Gabriel tensed for a moment as Megan released a contented sigh. The warmth of her embrace and her honest affection tore him apart. He needed her, needed her in his life, but how could he show her what he truly was?

A Feral—a savage, dangerous Draicon who had let down those who relied on him.

She must never know.

But the feel of her against him was so soft and good, he allowed himself the luxury of being loved without fear. Closing his eyes, Gabriel savored it as he would enjoy a long, leisurely meal. He cupped her face in his hands and gently brushed his lips against hers. Gabriel closed his eyes, tasting the sweetness on her mouth. He kissed her with light butterfly strokes as he heard her sigh. Then he deepened the kiss, his need boiling to the surface.

"The twins will be awake soon," she murmured.

He tightened his grip. "Not if I give them a little push to help them sleep."

"Normally I'd say no, but they do need their rest."

He broke the kiss, rubbed his temple. "That will do."

Turning off the heat beneath the frying pan, he then took her hand and led her back into the bedroom.

Flushed with joy and newly found sexuality, Megan sat at the table watching the twins and her mate dig into their breakfast. Gabriel caught her staring, winked.

The house's safety and cozy interior made her feel protected and comfortable. They were like a little family. She could indulge in the dream of her and Gabriel together like this, their own children chattering as they ate the meal he'd cooked....

Her coffee cup slammed down, spilling black liquid. Gabriel glanced up, wiped his mouth with a paper napkin.

"What is it?"

"The letter," she said tersely. "We forgot all about it."

The dreamy mood broke. Inside the sealed envelope was the objective of her quest. Megan dreaded opening it.

They had already suffered enough instability. She set the envelope before Gabriel, then went on her knees before the twins.

"Jenny, Jilly, whatever is inside that letter, I want you to know this. You'll always be my family and whenever you need me, wherever I am, and wherever you are, I'll be there for you. Okay? Nothing can break apart the Three Musketeers, not time or distance or a silly old letter."

"Four," Jillian whispered. "Four Musketeers. Don't forget Gabriel."

She met his solemn gaze. "Four. Gabriel. It's time."

Gabriel broke the red seal and began to read.

Then he looked up, his tanned, handsome face slack with shock.

"What is it?" she cried out.

"I can't believe this...."

Jillian and Jennifer were not strangers to him. They were his nieces. His flesh and blood. Alex's twins, the ones Simone had said were stillborn.

They were alive and sitting before him, staring at him with their mother's eyes.

Gabriel's mouth went dry as the paper fluttered to the table. Megan pressed his arm. "What is it? What did Gram say to Alexandre?"

Words lodged in his throat. Gabriel looked at Jenny and Jillian and his mind finally acknowledged what his heart knew all along. How they resembled their mother, her sweet heart-shaped face, her gentle innocence and shining belief in all things good.

"You're my nieces," he said thickly, hugging them tight. "My brother Alex's lost girls. We thought you were dead. Oh God, we were told you had died."

"You mean you're our uncle?" Jennifer asked.

"We have family," Jillian said happily. "You're really our uncle. I knew you were a real Musketeer!"

"You're my brother Alex's little girls. You have a dad." Overcome, he swallowed past the dryness in his throat and murmured to Megan as if seeing the girls anew. "Twins. *Ils se ressemblent comme deux gouttes d'eau.*"

They resemble each other like two drops of water.

Tears shimmered in Megan's eyes, tears he would never allow himself. The twins did not ask questions. They merely hugged him back.

Lifting his gaze to the girls, Gabriel made the first promise he'd uttered since the day Amelia died. "On my honor as a Draicon, I make you this vow," he said hoarsely. "I will get you to your dad. I swear, I don't care if it takes the last breath in my body. You'll be safe in my care until you at last get to meet your father. And he finally gets to hold you in his arms."

When he stood, he met Megan's shocked gaze. Gabriel pointed to the letter. His eyes were dryer than desert sand. Emotions roiled through him, but he brutally forced them aside.

"It's from Simone, written after the twins were born."

Watching her read the note, the knife in his heart twisted hard and sank deep. Simone had visited Shadow Island, the land of her birth, when she was pregnant and suddenly went into labor there.

The note explained the secret kept by Simone and her mother, who was Megan's grandmother. Jillian and Jennifer carried a distinctive Shadow birthmark. Simone had made the agonizing decision to leave the girls with her mother to raise because they would never be fully accepted by Alex's family, his pack, with their Shadow heritage.

Tears swam in Megan's big blue eyes as she carefully set down the paper. "She never knew that Shadow Island would become a prison. To Sissy, it was a refuge for her babies. Gabriel, they have a real father. Now I know they'll be in good hands with you by their side, too. You won't let anything happen to them."

"I have to go out," he muttered.

"Now? Gabriel, what's going on with you?"

"Nothing."

The door slammed behind him. He headed for the lake needing to be alone with his turbulent thoughts.

Gabriel was shutting her out again.

The twins came first. She hugged them, asked if they had any questions. They did, expressing their concern over their unknown father. Would he love them? Was he a good person who, even though he was Draicon, wouldn't make them feel bad the way other Draicon had?

"He's Gabriel's brother, remember? You like Gabriel, he's been good to you. I'm sure Alex will be just as brave and good as his brother."

But as secretive? She'd wanted a mate who wouldn't hide from her emotionally. Megan smiled to assuage their fears and told them to go clean up.

She ran water into the sink and began washing dishes. The closeness of last night caved into morning doubt. Would Gabriel ever fully open to her and bond with her emotionally instead of physically?

She needed all of him, not just the parts he chose to share with her.

Now she needed space. Megan set aside the dishes, grabbed a bottle of water and went outside into the sultry heat. The wood swing hanging from a large tree branch provided a perfect place to contemplate and relax.

At least now they knew the twins would never be alone. Megan smiled at the girls as they scampered outside, embarking on a furious game of tag.

"Cousin Megan?" Jennifer stopped. "Is it okay if we play hide-and-seek? There's no one around to see us."

"Why not? Just keep it to half an hour. Don't wear yourselves out."

Shrieking, the girls ran toward the forest. She tracked their scent, and settled back into the swing.

"Where are the girls?"

Gabriel joined her, thumbs hooked into his jeans, his long legs splayed before him. Megan shivered in pleasurable remembrance of the soft hairs on those limbs rubbing against hers as he thrust slowly inside her.

"Playing. They're fine. What about you?"

"I don't see them."

"Stop worrying, they're fine."

"They're my nieces now, my responsibility." He shaded his eyes. "I can scent them, but can't see them."

His expression darkened. "Jennifer is in the tree. *Merde. Descends del la droite maintenant!* Get down from there!"

Emerging from Shadow, Jennifer climbed down. Megan told them to keep playing.

"Gabriel, they're the same little girls they were an hour ago, before you read the letter," she reminded. "You've done a wonderful job making sure we are out of danger. Stop worrying."

"I can never stop worrying. It's like asking me to stop breathing." He stood up and whirled around as giggles surrounded them.

Anger dawned on his face. "They're in Shadow."

"Jennifer asked and I told her it was fine for them to play their favorite game, hide-and-seek." Megan listened as the laughing girls ran toward the woods.

"They shouldn't be. They have to keep their energy levels primed, not waste them on play."

As he started toward the forest after them, she leaped up and grabbed his arm. "What is it, Gabriel? Why are you like this all of the sudden?"

He halted, looking down at her hand on his arm. "I don't want anyone unprepared, not after what happened at the last house. We're still being followed and it's only time before we're found again."

"They're just little girls who need some normalcy, as you said last night," she pointed out. "Let them play."

"Play is fine. But not while using their powers."

"I told them only thirty minutes."

He walked over to the azalea bushes wreathing the tree trunk. She could not see his expression, but pain radiated from him like glowing embers.

Suddenly she knew he wasn't being authoritative about the twins because he was exercising his rights as a blood relative. He was worried about their safety.

"Thank you for looking after them. You risked a lot for them."

"I only wanted them to have as normal a

childhood as possible, despite the restrictions placed on us. They're good kids, Gabriel. They deserve to be loved. Doesn't everyone?"

Silence filled the space between them, broken by the twins' shrill laughs. "Some don't deserve love," he said finally.

Emotion clogged her throat. "Everyone does. Especially little boys who think they don't deserve it."

For a moment he stared into her eyes, his yearning evident. "You can trust me now, Gabriel. I will not betray you."

It seemed as if a connection had been made, bonding them together. Hope rose that maybe this could be the moment when he finally opened to her.

She waited. Gabriel leaned forward, his muscular forearms braced on his splayed knees. The sounds of the girls playing, squirrels chattering overhead and the distant caw of a crow rubbed against the silence between them. The heat was a sultry, living creature licking his spine and dampening his shirt. A bead of sweat condensed on his temple, rolled down his angular cheek.

Sensing his thirst, Megan handed him her water. He smiled his thanks. Gabriel tipped up the bottle. Fascination stole over her as she watched his strong throat muscles work.

He wiped his mouth with the back of one hand. Her gaze settled on that warm, wet mouth.

The bottle dropped to the ground as he cupped her face in his hands and kissed her deeply. Gabriel drew her closer and intensified the kiss, making her toes curl. Heat pooled between her legs.

A loud, frightened shriek broke them apart like two strong hands.

Megan shot to her feet as Gabriel bolted toward the woods. "Jilly, Jenny," he yelled. "Where are you? What's wrong?"

"Gabriel, help us! Something's got Jilly!"

He vanished into the woods. With each frenetic beat of her heart, Megan raced toward the screams.

Chapter 14

Panic sliced through Megan as she saw her cousin.

Jennifer was on the ground, trying to shake the tree. Her sister was on the outstretched limb, struggling to free herself from the grip of…

Pure terror seized Megan.

The green-scaled creature was nine feet long, its pointed teeth sinking into Jillian's ankle. Her cousin screamed in fear and pain as she tried to pull free.

"Jillian, stay there, don't move! I'm coming up. If you move, sweetheart, you'll hurt yourself more."

Gabriel began to climb. From limb to limb he moved, strong and sure. Megan ran over to Jennifer, hugged her cousin.

Blood began to drip from the tree limb holding Jillian.

Sickened, Megan wished she could do something. She could not shift into wolf, only Shadow. And being invisible would not help her cousin.

She could only hold Jennifer as Gabriel approached the scaled beast. Jillian screamed in pain.

"Hang on, Jilly," Gabriel told her softly. "I need for you to be still. I know it hurts like the dickens, sweetie, but in order to free you, you have to be still."

"Okay," she sobbed.

"That's my brave girl. Megan, get under that branch and be ready to catch her when I give the word."

As she blinked, Gabriel pounced on the creature. He landed on its back and with his hands, forced open the powerful jaws.

"Now, Jilly, drop!"

Trusting in him, Jillian fell to the ground. Megan caught her little cousin. Her right ankle was bleeding badly.

They glanced up to see Gabriel wrestling with

the creature, his hands locked as he broke its neck with a single, sickly crack.

She shuddered at the killing power of those hands, hands that had been so gentle on her body just hours ago.

"Stand back. I'm coming down."

Gabriel dropped to the ground fifteen feet below, landing on his feet like a cat.

"What was it?" Megan asked, gripping the weeping Jillian.

"A damned alligator. Here, give her to me. I'll carry her."

She handed over his injured niece. "They don't climb trees!"

"Morphs in gator form do."

He hurried into the house with the crying Jillian, hushing her as he cradled her close. "It's okay, sweetheart. I've got you. You're okay now."

On the sofa, Gabriel gently laid down Jillian and carefully examined her ankle. "Not broken, but she's got some deep cuts."

Megan cleaned her cousin's wounds, worried that Jillian didn't protest as usual with her "Ow, that hurts!"

She applied the healing liniment, bound her

bleeding ankle. Gabriel handed her cousin an aspirin and Jillian gulped it down with the water her twin handed her.

Pack up, Megan. We're leaving as soon as we can. It's not safe here any longer.

How did the Morph get on the property? You shielded it against Morphs.

Against them breaking in. These were already here.

A hollow ache settled on her chest as she tossed things into her large backpack. The fragile, pretty Dresden figurine sat on the bureau. Megan picked it up, stroking the china face. It was all she had of her mother's.

For two precious days, this place had been a home where children played and a family gathered at the dinner table. She'd imagined making a life in such a place with Gabriel, where she wouldn't have to run anymore.

Megan folded the figurine into a towel and stuffed it carefully into her knapsack.

She was homeless once more.

Gabriel stomped inside. "I grabbed all the girls' stuff and mine, threw everything in the trunk. You almost ready?"

She handed him her pack. "Just this. Oh, and I wanted to bring some of those fresh bananas and strawberries you bought. The girls love them."

"Hurry up."

The kitchen was cozy and neat. She tasted tears in the back of her throat as she touched the gingham curtains, the matching tablecloth. "I'm so damn tired of running. Will it ever stop? Will we ever be safe?"

A hissing sounded close to the kitchen door. Gas leak? Megan inhaled and caught an odor of decaying flesh. Edging aside the checked curtain, she peered out the backdoor window.

Nothing. Megan unlocked the door to go outside. Something plopped to the hardwood floor besides her.

The hissing grew louder. Terror seized her heart as her palms grew cold and clammy.

A scream tore from her throat as the rattler lifted its head to strike. Instinctively she went into Shadow and sidestepped. Megan danced away. Horrified, she saw another snake poke a hole in the ceiling and drop through.

They were coming through the roof.

Shifting out of Shadow, she ran into the living room, yanked Jennifer off the sofa. "Run for the car."

As she picked up Jillian in her arms, she glanced over her shoulder.

Hundreds of snakes and spiders dropped into the kitchen, slithering and crawling toward them. Megan dashed outside the front door with the twins and ground to an abrupt halt.

The yard was filled with snakes. Jenny screamed as she ran, barely missing a cobra snapping at her heels. Gabriel swept her up into his arms and all but threw her into the car.

By the time he turned back, snakes covered the yard. Megan and Jillian were trapped between the porch and the car.

Megan could feel a spider climb up her bare ankle, pause delicately with its whisper thin legs. She shook it off.

Gabriel advanced toward the house. Determination etched his face.

"I'm coming out." The snakes would bite her, but Jillian would stay safe.

"Stay there, Megan, until I give the word."

Astonishment filled her as she watched him

stretch out his hands. Could he mind control hundreds of Morph snakes?

In the midst of the mass of writhing reptiles, something began growing. Sensing a predator larger than themselves, the snakes backed away.

Dust and earth swirled in a violent vortex, clogging the air. Then the cloud cleared. Gabriel walked forward, wind whipping back his hair as he held out his hands. Power radiated from him.

A python as big as a palm tree raised itself until its triangular head reached the rooftop. Out of a huge, yawning mouth flicked a forked tongue as the snake hissed at the intruding Morphs.

The rattlers and cobras retreated, clearing a small pathway.

Gabriel reached the porch, swept Megan and Jillian into his arms. She gripped Jilly tighter as her cousin buried her head against her neck. It was real, yet it wasn't.

His arms were strong and secure. Skin stretched tightly over his cheekbones in harsh relief as he marched toward the car. Megan's heart gave a sickening lurch as they skirted the python. *It's just his magick, his magick, not real...*

When he set them down, Megan settled Jillian inside the car and watched from the safety of the vehicle as the python illusion vanished. Amber ignited Gabriel's gaze as he held out his hands. Streaks of blackness began flowing from the snakes and spiders. Flowing into him.

A cruel, icy smile touched his mouth. "Go to hell," he ordered.

A blast of white-hot light shot from his outstretched hands. The Morphs shattered in a boiling black explosion. She shielded her eyes against it.

When she opened her eyes, all that was left were piles of gray ash.

He had siphoned the energy from the Morphs, reversed it and turned it against them. Never had she witnessed such power. Megan shrank back in awe.

Gabriel was far more lethal than she'd realized.

No one spoke as Gabriel drove west on Highway 60. Her face blanched, Megan sat in the front seat, gripping the door handle. As if she were ready to spring out, or break it off and use it as a weapon.

He swore silently. Knew how scary it was to others when he used all his powers, but he'd had no choice. If he shifted, he knew he could not control the beast. The beast would have made short work of all the snakes, but its savagery would have terrified Megan and the twins more than the energy reversal.

Glancing over, he was startled to realize Megan was invisible. A hollow ache settled in his chest. Shadows did that when they felt frightened and trapped.

It wasn't his wolf intimidating her. It was him.

Gabriel turned at a small, hesitant tap on his right shoulder.

"Uncle Gabriel? You left this on the backseat. I thought you'd want it."

The black Stetson pushed between the seat opening.

A half smile touched his mouth. "Thanks, hon." He clapped it on his head, saw her awed expression. "Now, see? I'm the same Gabriel, the one who takes you fishing on the lake and makes you take baths."

Tension on their faces eased the slightest bit.

But Megan remained in Shadow. Had to show her there was nothing scary about him….

Liar, the voice inside him whispered.

"It's just me, Megan," he said gently. "I'm not the one who would ever hurt you."

Form shimmered and then took shape. Megan pressed against the door, but at least she was visible once more.

"How…" She cleared her throat. "How did you do that?"

"Something I learned from Emily, my sister-in-law. She has special abilities. Emily showed me to harness my powers to destroy Morphs. I siphon their negative energy, take it into my body, create white light to destroy them."

"Reverse energy transmutation. It takes a very powerful Draicon to do that. I've never seen anything like it," she whispered.

Fear leeched from her pores. "I did it to protect you, Megan."

"What else are you capable of, Gabriel? What

kind of Draicon are you? When we fully bond, what powers will we exchange?"

The closeness they'd shared while making love vanished like water in the desert. He could not answer her.

He did not dare.

Opening his senses, he smelled Megan's floral fragrance, his own scent wrapped possessively around hers now that they'd made love. The fresh vanilla scent of the twins. Gasoline, and a faint odor of something darker, nasty lying underneath. His nostrils flared.

"Megan, do you smell that? Burning plastic and sour wine."

Closing her eyes, she inhaled. "Something spilled in the car?"

"Or worse. Someone was in here."

He kept an eye on the rearview mirror. Traffic was light, except for a sleek silver pickup truck gaining on them fast.

Gabriel pressed down the gas pedal. The speedometer inched up. Megan craned her neck and looked back. Her fingers gripped the headrest. "That truck wants to pass us."

Now the truck filled his rearview mirror. He caught sight of the driver's face.

A driver with silver hair.

"Oh God, Gabriel. It's him."

Panic flared on Megan's face. The taste of it burned in his mouth, along with the acid triumph of the man chasing them.

The truck banged into his bumper, jerking them forward. The girls cried out.

Behind them, the truck pulled off the road. Waiting, like a giant black spider. Gabriel swore and pressed the gas pedal to the floor, but the vehicle only slowed. The pungent odor of spilt gasoline filled the air as the gauge flipped down to empty. The car had been sabotaged. They were screwed.

"Not on my watch, you bastard," he muttered.

The stench grew thick and oily. Their pursuer wanted to make damn sure they were paralyzed.

The Chevy slowed to a crawl. Gabriel coaxed the engine to keep going, then pulled off the roadside. The engine died with a cough. The odor of gasoline clogged his nostrils as he got out. He slid under the car and swore.

Gravel and dirt coated the back of his jeans and T-shirt as he slid out. Dusting them off, Gabriel got inside the vehicle.

"Fuel line's loosened, enough to let us get away. The bastard's toying with us." He swung his head around, saw the truck pull onto the road again. Toward them. The enemy was gaining.

"Megan, cloak the car."

The glamour turned the vehicle and its occupants invisible.

In the rearview mirror, confusion filled the expression of their pursuer. Buying them a little time. Just a little.

"We can't stay here forever." Megan stared at the approaching truck.

"I know. Jilly, Jenny, remember what I said about using your powers? Listen carefully, *mes petites.* I need your help."

The truck slowed and passed them. Chasing an invisible car. *Good luck, you bastard.*

"Just until we reach the turnpike, honey. There's a motel there where I can find another car. Can you do it?"

Blood drained from Jenny's face but she gave a brave nod.

"Hang tight, everyone."

Power hummed. The car still cloaked in Shadow inched out onto the road and then moved forward. The engine remained shut off. Jenny was now its motor.

Gabriel tensed as they gained on the truck. Strain lined Jenny's face as she corralled her magick to propel them forward.

"Keep her steady forward, Jenny. Faster. I'm going to pass him."

Gabriel eased the Chevy into the other lane. As they began to pass the truck, he studied the face of his enemy, imprinting it into his mind.

The pale features were etched with hatred. The silver-haired man raised a hand. Claws erupted from the fingertips. Snarling, the man reached out and shredded the seat beside him.

They pulled in front of the truck and Jenny pushed the car faster. Megan watched in the mirror as the truck pulled off the side of the road.

"Draicon," Gabriel said in a low voice. "One of us. He'll follow our scent trail, so we're not free yet. But we have enough of a start because he's searching for us back there."

He praised Jenny for her talents, coaxing her to keep up the constant flow of magick. Eyes closed, Jenny held out her hands as she pushed the car to eighty.

"No one on the road. Now, Megan. Uncloak the car."

When they reached the motel by the Florida Turnpike entrance, he steered the car toward the back parking lot. "Stay here," he ordered.

Minutes later, a burgundy SUV pulled up beside the Chevy. Gabriel slid out, dangling keys from his lean fingers.

"GMC Grand Terrain, only 3,000 miles on it, full tank of gas, just purchased for $50,000. The money will be wired to the man's account."

"You mind pushed him."

"More than fair deal. Besides, he's not eager to get home from his sales trip. His wife is mad at him for buying the new SUV when they needed the money to repair their roof." Gabriel handed over her backpack as they carried the bags to the vehicle. "I chose him because I figured you'd feel empathy for his wife, roof leak and all."

She held out her hands for the keys. "Let me drive."

He cocked his head, but handed over the keys.

It wasn't until they were heading north on the Turnpike that Megan finally relaxed a little. Gabriel smiled at the pale-faced Jenny. "You did great, sweetheart. You're a real Robichaux, just like your daddy. Rise to the occasion and come through when you're needed. We'll stop at the next rest stop and get you some food to replenish your energy."

Glowing under his praise, Jenny beamed.

"What about me?" Jillian demanded.

"You did fine, too. Jenny needed her sister for support. That's what family's all about. Sometimes one of you does what's necessary and the other is there to encourage."

Megan gave him a long, thoughtful look as he turned around. "You're really good with children. I know you'll make a great father."

Gabriel leaned back, slid the cowboy hat down on his face. "Children are out of the question, Megan."

His words caused a crushing hurt in her chest. "Because of me, because of my Shadow powers? You don't want a child who might inherit them, just like your brother didn't?"

"Leave my brother out of this."

"It's me, then. My powers."

"It's not you and I'm not talking about this anymore. Let's just get the hell to New Orleans."

At his curt attitude, she stopped talking. Megan flipped on a satellite radio station. Alternative rock filled the vehicle.

Gabriel shot her a questioning look. She ignored him, but couldn't do the same with the tightness in her chest. He kept shutting her out, time and again. She was mated to him. They'd consummated their bond, yet he was no closer to her than when they'd first met.

A cell phone chirped. Gabriel fished his out of his front pocket. He frowned at the number. It kept ringing.

The way he kept glancing at the screen didn't give her confidence. He flipped the phone open. "Robichaux," he bit out.

Blood drained from his face. He gripped the

phone tighter. Megan's heart raced at the stark fury on his expression.

"Feet pue tan," he snapped.

The meaning flashed loud inside her mind. *You goddamn son of a bitch.*

The phone cracked in his hands. Gabriel tossed the pieces aside. White lined his knuckles as his mouth narrowed to a thin slash.

"Was it him?"

A low growl rumbled from his chest. Her stomach tightened into knots. The flash of anger across his face made him look edgy and dangerous. Gabriel took in a deep breath.

"Who's he after? The girls? Or is he a mercenary who wants to take me back the colony? What does he want, Gabriel?"

Dark silence fell in the vehicle for a minute. Then Gabriel pushed back his hat. She could see the haunted look in his chocolate eyes.

"He's not after you or the twins. It's me he wants, Megan. Me."

Chapter 15

"Gabriel, Jenny's not feeling well."

The small voice coming from the backseat understated the problem. Jennifer was pale, her energy depleted to alarming levels.

He spotted a sign for a rest stop a few miles ahead and told Megan. Her rounded chin had that stubborn set he'd begun to recognize as sheer will.

"He's not going to get you, Gabriel. We can stop him."

His heart turned over at her obvious loyalty. "I won't risk you or the twins. This is my business and I'm responsible."

"They can't take you away for protecting Shadows. If you hadn't helped us..."

"That's not why he's after me." An ache settled deep in his bones. "His name is Logan Hartwell. I've never met him, but knew his son, Deke."

"Friends?"

"Hardly."

He could be the most powerful Draicon walking the planet and it didn't matter. Gabriel rubbed his chest. *Merde,* it was hard to breathe, hard to think….

Hard to live with the twin boulders of guilt always weighing him down. One on his shoulder named Amelia. One named Simone.

Daring to glance sideways, he saw compassion on Megan's face.

"Tell me," she said.

Seeing the exit for the service plaza, she pulled into the left lane. People streamed back and forth in the busy plaza. After she parked the SUV, she turned off the engine.

A small white van with pictures of creamy treats was parked nearby. Jenny brightened. Gabriel fished out dollar bills from his wallet.

"Jenny, Jilly, *alors,* here's a few dollars. Go

get ice cream, *mes petites.* Stay where I can keep an eye on you."

He watched the girls scramble out and walk hand in hand toward the truck.

"Who are you, Gabriel?"

The question laced with bite like Tabasco. Megan waited.

"Sometimes, I don't even know" was his honest answer.

Gabriel took a deep breath. Oh damn, this hurt so bad. "Like I'd said before, I was a cocky, arrogant *feet pue tan...*"

He halted, removed his hat, jammed a hand through his thick hair. Couldn't tell her, not like this, not ever. The haunting image of Simone's dead eyes, Amelia's frozen scream of terror.

Then he felt Megan's gentle caress on his forearm.

"I was an Enforcer, who formed the network with Alex. I helped Shadows personally, escorted them to safe houses. I myself recruited the Friends who'd help Shadows find refuge. One day, I made a critical mistake. I trusted someone."

"Deke?"

"He came to me as an escaped Shadow, asking for refuge. Remy didn't trust him. Sensed something a little off. Should have listened to him. I thought Papa's dislike for Shadows overtook all else. Deke was desperate. I invited him into Alex's home to spend the night while I made arrangements to find a safe house. Alex agreed."

His jaw clenched so hard his teeth hurt. "That night, Deke had dinner with all of us at Alex's house so Simone could convince my parents Shadows were worth saving. Simone had forgotten dessert, so she asked my parents to get ice cream from the local store. It was a ploy. She'd asked me for a favor, to use my powers and coax my brothers into leaving with my parents."

Shame etched his face. Gabriel dragged in a deep breath. "Rafe is immune to my powers, but he went because he sensed we needed to talk freely. We were alone, Simone, Amelia, Alex, Deke and myself. Amelia was bursting with curiosity. Deke was the first Shadow she'd seen other than her mother. She was so honest, told Deke how her mommy was a Shadow and was teaching her how to use her talents. She was so excited to meet another Shadow."

"He wasn't?" Megan's face drained of color.

"No." Gabriel's chest felt tight. "Found out later he was an Enforcer."

Her mouth trembled. "Oh God."

"Deke asked Amelia and Simone to step outside and talk, Shadow to Shadow. Alex had gone upstairs. I was on my laptop writing emails. My instincts were warning me. I shut off the computer but by then I could hear…"

The screams.

The crescents of his clipped nails dug into his palms. Must keep going, because if he stopped, the tide of emotions would engulf him.

Or scream himself, and never stop. He took a cleansing breath, craned his neck to see the girls still standing in line for ice cream.

"The rest of the family had returned and ran outside. Simone and Amelia were dying. Rafe tried to save them, he's the immortal Kallan and had the gift to restore life to one dying person. He asked Alex to choose which to save, the mother or the child. Alex couldn't choose." Gabriel stared at the radio, unwilling to meet her gaze. "We buried them two days later. Alex… has never been the same."

Neither have I.

Simone and Amelia prone on the ground, gasping for breath. A bloodstained Deke grinning as he held the knife he'd grabbed from their kitchen. The slow, viscous river of crimson pooling at Gabriel's boots.

"What did you do, Gabriel?"

Her gentle, melodic voice a stroke of silk against raw nerves. Gabriel stared at his hands.

"I grabbed the knife from him, dragged Deke away while Alex held Simone and Amelia in his arms, rocking back and forth."

"Deke?" The word was a horrified whisper.

"Made sure he was dead."

Deke, backing away in terror. Gabriel lunging forward, shape-shifting as he ran.

"What happened?"

For a long moment the only sounds were the slamming of car doors, the insouciant chatter of travelers and the grumble of passing tractor trailers.

"I went Feral."

The image surfaced like a bloated body

slowly floating upward from a dark, deep lake. Megan slipped into his mind. He tried to shut her out, but the door had cracked open.

He'd torn the bastard's throat raw. And more. Blood on the trees, the grass. The horrified looks of his family when he'd emerged from the woods. Blood splattered over his naked body. Unable to control his magick to even clothe himself. Their fear. He could never forgive himself for the look in their eyes. His own family.

Silence, then the thunder of a pounding heartbeat. A small, choked sound beside him. A fist of guilt and regret slammed into his chest. He wouldn't look at her, see her revulsion.

"Rafe and Etienne buried what was left of him, circulated a story about Deke torn to pieces by a wolf." He gave a short, bitter laugh. His brothers had told the truth.

"No mercy, Gabriel."

He dared to glance up. Blue fire raged in her eyes.

"Deke deserved no mercy," she repeated.

The sharp pain in his chest eased a bit. "Logan didn't believe the planted story. He's discovered the truth. All of it. He wants my hide. And you and the girls are a bonus. I'll be damned if he touches you."

The hand he ran over his cheek scrubbed lengthening bristles. Fingernails began elongating into claws. Gabriel fisted his hands. "Go see to the girls, Megan. I'll be out in a minute."

He fought the change, his wolf snarling to escape. Fur rippled along his arms, covered the backs of his hands. The tight, itching feeling burst out of his chest.

Minutes passed. He gave a short, bitter laugh at the people rushing in and out of the service plaza. If they knew a werewolf was in the car, ready to spring out and release all the savagery inside him, would they be so cavalier?

Logan's cold voice echoed in his mind. "I'll be waiting for you in New Orleans, Robichaux. When I'm finished with you, I'll drag your sorry carcass to the council, along with the Shadows, and get the reward for killing the disgusting animal you are. If I were you, I wouldn't stop to rest before you reach the city."

Cold panic raced through him. Stop to rest…

He whipped his head toward the ice cream truck.

It was gone.

"Megan!" The name came out in a snarl.

Couldn't leave the car like this, too many people and he needed to reserve his power. Gabriel glanced at his arms and whispered, "Stop it." Thoughts of home and family didn't hold the wolf at bay.

Megan's sweet smile flashed before him. Gabriel slowly unclenched his fists.

Fur had vanished from his hands and arms. He bolted out of the car, raced across the parking lot toward the plaza. Gabriel hooked a left around the plaza's building and ground to a halt.

On the southbound side of the plaza, the parking lot had emptied and no traffic zipped past on the Turnpike. Complete quiet.

Except for the merry tinkling of an ice cream truck. It ground on his sensitive eardrums like broken glass as it rolled toward him.

Fifty yards away, he saw the driver's yellow eyes flash pure black. Soulless.

Morph.

Gray, mottled skin like a corpse's. Wisps of hair tufted from its sunken scalp. The creature stopped the truck, slid out and faced Gabriel with an obscene giggle. It dragged itself closer. A stench of rotting flesh drifted on the air.

"Where are they?" he demanded.

"Safe, oh so safe. The master wants them for dessert. But you, you're the entrée. My entrée."

The creature's razor thin voice lowered to a raw whisper. "I'll rip out your heart and suck out your energy, Draicon. You'll die with your entrails in my mouth. And I'll make them… watch."

Testosterone levels shot up. His body hardened to a steel blade, ready to cut and dice and chop. His beast growled in approval.

Then he glanced at the service window of the truck, where children had handed over dollar bills in exchange for treats. Frozen in terror, Jennifer and Jillian stared out at him. Squares of silver duct tape sealed their mouths shut.

The Morph raised a hand and flicked a talon at them.

"Such simple, sweet children. So easy to cork their magick. Just one swipe of their cousin's cheek and a small lick of her blood and they screamed for me to stop. They begged."

Megan's face appeared in the window, her wild gaze boring into his. Dry lips moved past the dirty gag shoved into her mouth.

Gabriel hesitated.

A gnashing, whirling sound drew closer. The Morph had shifted and cloned itself into a pack of wolves. Not ordinary wolves. White foam dribbled from their sharp teeth.

Rabid wolves.

The frantic beat of a terrified heart as he'd dismembered, slowly, oh so slowly, Deke as the Draicon screamed. White splinters of bone, coated with blood as Gabriel had bitten off his left femur and tossed it aside like a dog discarded an unwanted toy....

The thought of her seeing his wolf emerge and go Feral made his stomach churn. He called forth his magick, drew on the Morph blackness, siphoned it inside him.

Gabriel flung out his hands at the snarling horde, but the pack parted. The energy bolt slammed into the ice cream truck, obliterating the front grill and shattering the windshield. Screams erupted inside.

Merde, he would kill them. Couldn't transmute the energy. Gabriel backed off the magick, sent it hurling toward a lamppost. It exploded in a shower of steel sparks.

Two dozen wolves with bared teeth faced him. Reckless courage filled him. Standing straight and proud, he extended both middle fingers at the wolf pack.

"Embrasse moi tchew," he told them. *Kiss my ass.*

The Morphs fell on him.

Mustering all his strength, he charged forward again, ignoring the demanding howl of his beast to be freed.

Gabriel was going to die out there.

Megan struggled to loosen the ropes binding her. Her first concern after awakening from the vicious blow had been soothing the girls' terrors. Now, seeing her mate bloodied as the pack of snarling wolves tore into him, anger swelled inside her.

The ropes burst apart with brute strength. Megan tore the gag from her mouth, leaned toward the girls and ripped off the duct tape.

She found the key, unlocked the silver handcuffs that inhibited their magick.

"Stay here," she ordered the twins. "If anything happens to Gabriel or me, use your magick. Find a ride, use glamour and get to New Orleans."

She kissed their tear-dampened cheeks and burst outside. Spreading her fingers, Megan let the magick gather inside her.

Halfling Shadows had a little secret few knew about. As if to make up for their deficit, the goddess had endowed her with a special ability. She rarely used it.

She used it now. Megan sent energy hurling outward.

Dozens of snarling wolves popped out of thin air. Wolves the size of Lincoln Continentals with teeth long as carving knives. The Morphs halted their attack on Gabriel and turned around. They howled as her pack of wolves raced forward.

Megan smiled. Aggression had its uses.

The Morphs snarled in fear, backing away from this new threat. Their retreat gave Gabriel a needed advantage. He crouched into a fighting stance as a Morph attacked one of her wolves.

As Morph talons touched the wolf's fur, the lupine vanished. She could swear the Morph looked confused. As the other Morph clones engaged her Shadow clones, Gabriel attacked from the rear. A scream of raw fury tearing from her throat, Megan charged forward. The scream turned into a growl.

She leaped on the closest Morph with fangs and teeth and claws. Acid blood spurted, but she ignored the splash as it sank into her thick fur. When the Morph lay dead at her feet, it vanished into a pile of gray ash.

The rest of the Morphs were dead by Gabriel's hand. Megan glanced out of her wolf eyes at her mate. Covered in blood, Gabriel had several raw wounds where the Morphs had gouged out skin. He sank to his knees, bending over and wheezing.

He was hurt, badly. Why hadn't he released his wolf?

Concern filled her. Suddenly she found herself standing on two legs. Megan waved a hand

and clothed herself. She raced forward, dropped to the ground beside Gabriel.

Blood streamed from a deep gash in his forehead. Tenderly, she wiped back a hank of dark hair hanging over his brow. Gabriel looked up through half-lowered lids.

"What was that?" he rasped.

"A little trick of mine. Shadow clones. They look real, act real, until you touch them."

Her arms went around him, holding him tight. For a long while they remained like that, until Gabriel raised his head. His gaze was sharpened, renewed with determination.

"Go get the girls, and let's get out of here."

"Shouldn't you rest first? You're wounded."

"No time. I'll be fine." He stood, shrugging off her assistance. "No time."

Megan glanced at the piles of gray ash, already blown by the wind. On the turnpike, a few cars went southbound once more, the accident created by the Morphs now clearing up.

"But Gabriel, the Morphs are dead."

"Logan isn't. And he won't stop until I am."

Chapter 16

"Why didn't you shift?" Megan asked.

On the seat beside her, Gabriel didn't reply. They'd bandaged the worst of his wounds and already he'd started to heal. He flexed his bruised right hand and gave his fingertips a wry look.

"Damn energy sucking *couillon*. Ruined my manicure. Now I'll have to get another."

"Gabriel, it isn't funny."

"I know. Manicures are damn expensive."

"Your wolf could have defeated them without you getting so injured. Why didn't you shift?" Megan passed a slow-moving RV. Children staring out of one window saw the twins in the backseat and waved. The girls gave a sluggish wave back. The Morphs had not injured them, but their listless attitudes worried her.

Gabriel's insouciance about his injuries was also bothersome. He hid something dangerous.

He tipped his hat down on his brow, shadowing his eyes. "Think I'll rest a bit. When you reach the next exit, get off. We need to eat and find a retail store."

"Not a nail salon?"

He gave an amused snort. "I've a hankering for a rare roast beef sandwich, first."

"I have a hankering, too. For answers. Why didn't you shift? I saw you throw the power surge."

She felt him go still. "That could have killed you and the girls."

Megan's voice softened. "But your wolf is your natural defense against Morphs. Your best chance of evening the fight."

"Not with me," he said darkly.

"Gabriel, what are you hiding from me? Why can't you trust me with the truth?"

"Some people can't handle the truth."

"I'm not one of them," she insisted. "I'm your

bonded mate. Are you thinking I'm too afraid to handle the truth?"

"Pas, maintenant," he said gently. "Of course not. One day, when things settle down, I'll tell you."

Then he tipped his hat down farther. "I'm getting some shut-eye. Wake me up when we get to Gainesville."

The deep, even sound of his breathing told her that he'd fallen asleep. Gabriel's ability to shut down to heal his injuries was as honed as his skills at shutting out her questions. She'd get no answers from him now.

Megan wondered if she ever would.

The steak dinner was delicious, but Megan had eaten purely to regain lost energy. His injuries healing quickly, Gabriel had washed up in the bathroom and changed into gray linen trousers and a hunter-green polo shirt. The preppy clothing stripped away the casual, earthy look Megan adored.

Now her stomach churned as they walked through a large retail store. The twins lagged behind them as he headed for the electronics section. Gabriel pulled two inexpensive cell phones from the shelves.

"The phones I'll toss out after I make a call. Those Morphs knew exactly where we were headed. Logan must have put a tracer on my cell and tracked us that way."

"Unless he tracked us by sound alone." Megan touched the plastic covering to the cell phone. "When I had mercenaries on my trail, they used vibrant echoes of my own voice to track me down. They had voice recognition scanners that could read and distinguish an individual's sound patterns."

"Impressive equipment. I doubt Logan is so sophisticated. He prefers more sedate, insidious ways of catching victims. Such as Morphs." Gabriel's gaze went icy and hard. "He's embraced evil to clone himself. He's Morph now, a Draicon's greatest threat."

"I thought Shadows were the greatest threat." Megan bit her lip at his darkened expression. "Why wouldn't other Draicon track and capture him, then?"

"His magick is powerful and ancient. He throws up enough glamour to fool most

Draicon. I didn't even know it was him until he called," Gabriel admitted.

He studied the twins examining the items on the shelves. His look softened. "There's a few more things I need to buy."

In the toy aisle, even the plethora of colorful electronic playthings didn't stir Jillian and Jennifer's interest. Only when Gabriel handed them each a blond doll did they brighten.

As they headed for women's clothing, her throat tightened at how the twins hugged their new treasures. The sooner they reached their father and had a secure home, the better. But would Alexandre love them, even though they were Shadows? Could Alexandre learn to reach out and share his world with Shadows?

The girls settled against a wall and glanced around. When no one looked, they vanished into Shadow.

"Stay here," Megan whispered. "Remember to cloak your scent, too. You'll be safe."

Women openly stared at him with feminine interest as Gabriel thumbed through the dress racks. Ignoring them, he chose a flowing dress with cap sleeves in a bright turquoise floral print. She hungered for such a pretty thing.

When she emerged from the dressing room and pivoted for his assessment, she felt feminine and aware. A man whistled at her. Crimson flooded her cheeks at the stranger's admiring gaze.

Frowning, Gabriel selected a sedate long-sleeved shirt and dressy black pants. "Try these on."

Gazing longingly at the dress, she shook her head. "I like this."

"It won't do for our next stop, *ma petite chou*."

While the endearment warmed her, Megan continued to look at the dress. Suddenly all she wanted was to look pretty, instead of a worn, desperate Shadow on the run. Gabriel cupped her chin, his touch sending heat shivering through her. "I need your legs and arms free for fighting."

"I can shift for that," she challenged.

His expression hardened again, reminding her of the ruthless Gabriel. "I won't see you tied up and gagged in another ice cream truck, Megan.

If you find yourself in a tight spot, you need every advantage. Now, go try them on."

The clothing fit perfectly. Gabriel trailed her back into the dressing room's tight confines. "You're so beautiful."

She warmed under his praise and laced her fingers through his in a simple act of trust. Megan squeezed his sun-darkened hand.

"Every woman in the store stared at you, Gabriel. They all want you."

He touched her cheek, the smooth stroke of his fingers creating a delicious friction. "I only see you, *ma petite chou.* Only you."

She started to undress.

"Wear them out," he instructed.

"But the tags…"

Lethally sharp claws emerged from his fingertips and Gabriel ripped off the tags. Stunned, she stared at his reflection in the mirror as he stood behind her. Unbuttoning the blouse, he slid it off her shoulders and pressed a sizzling kiss to her skin. Breath sucked in as he unhooked her lacy white bra and slid it off.

When his palms slid up to cup her breasts, her nipples tightened to hard diamonds. Need raged through her as his thumbs stroked. She reached behind her, slipped her hands down the front of his tight jeans and squeezed playfully.

A low growl escaped him.

He pressed against her backside, letting her feel the long length of his erection. Gabriel nuzzled her neck, his warm breath feathering over her cheek. Excitement bloomed hot and sharp in her belly.

"I want you, now," he breathed.

Turning her around, he stripped the pants off her and yanked down her white lace panties. Gabriel dropped to his knees and looked up at her. Intensity radiated in his amber gaze.

"Part your legs."

The rough order made her tremble. Megan leaned back against the coolness of the wall mirror as he pulled her close.

He put his mouth between her thighs. She bit back a scream as his tongue swept over her core.

The feelings were too much, too intense. *I can't bear it,* she moaned in his mind.

You can.

An excited whimper escaped her. Voices outside the dressing room warned they weren't alone. Someone banged on the dressing room door.

Gabriel's long fingers tightened as he continued tasting her.

"Is anyone in here?"

Panic shot through her pleasure. She glanced down and saw someone drop down to peer inside the room.

Yanking on her powers, she cloaked them in Shadow. Gabriel's scent swam in her nostrils. Her head lolled back, hips rising and falling to the erotic rhythm Gabriel created with his mouth.

Megan fisted her hands in his silky hair, anchoring to him. The hot tension built with each lash of his wicked tongue until she shattered, putting a fist at her mouth to hold back the screams.

Trembling, she eased her grip on him.

Seductive intent gleamed in his amber gaze as he stood, backhanding his wet mouth. Drawing in a trembling breath, Megan grasped his jeans. He made a rough sound as she caressed the long, hard length of him. Gabriel arched against her touch.

Emboldened by his desire, she unzipped him. He pushed the jeans past his lean hips, baring his thick erection. Lifting her by her bare bottom with one hand, he fisted the other in her long hair and kissed her deeply. She tasted the musk of her own arousal.

His cock nudged at her soaked folds. With an impatient sound, he pushed hard and deep inside her. Her inner walls shuddered and stretched to accommodate his invasion. She moaned into his mouth as he stroked his tongue inside.

Megan wrapped her legs around his hips as he began to thrust hard and deep. Gabriel pulled back, staring into her eyes. The intimate visual caress combined with his complete penetration built the tension higher and higher.

She reached down and licked the straining tendons of his neck, then lightly bit.

Snarling, he thrust harder, and she felt herself spiraling out of control. With a low moan, she climaxed as he buried his face into her shoulder. She felt him shudder, his hot seed flooding inside her.

The glamour faded, leaving them visible. Dazed with sensual pleasure, she trembled as he kissed her. Gabriel leaned his forehead against hers, his ragged breaths mingling with her own.

His eyes darkened to midnight. "Remember, Megan. You're mine."

He'd stamped his mark on her with the sharp point of sensual pleasure. After a few minutes, he pulled free. Megan dressed as he pulled up his jeans and donned his hat.

He put a possessive hand on the small of her back and ushered her out of the dressing room.

When they gathered the girls and checked out, she saw him slip the little floral dress onto the conveyer belt. A bolt of pleasure shot through her at his thoughtfulness.

In the car, Gabriel took a small chip from his wallet, inserted it into the new cell phone and made a quick call. Afterward, the phone crumbled to bits in his palm. He tossed the pieces aside.

"We're headed to a house where we'll rest

before leaving for the city. I don't like how quiet the girls have been."

"No place is safe," she countered.

"This place is. It belongs to Tristan. He's a Phoenix."

At her blank look, he added, "An Immortal Justice Guardian. You've never heard of them?"

"I thought they were myth. Just like Draicon justice is a myth. If such powerful creatures exist, why are my people still treated like outcasts?"

His jaw tightened. "They have a habit of not interfering with destiny. But when they do act, trust me, you don't want to get in their way."

"And how did you come into contact with this one? Did he help you out?"

A humorless smile touched his full mouth. "Hardly. Tristan beat me severely when I was much younger." He started the vehicle. "But he made me a promise. He told me if I ever truly needed him, I could call in a favor. Any favor."

"You're calling it in now?"

Gabriel fell silent for a moment. "For you, Megan. You're all that matters now. You and getting the twins safely to their father."

He'd sacrificed something that huge for her. Tightness gathered in her chest.

"Thank you, Gabriel. For everything."

Silence greeted her, but she sensed his enormous and fierce pride, his deep protective streak.

"How did you meet this Tristan?"

"It was a long time ago. I did something that warranted punishment."

She tried to imagine anything a young, carefree and cheerful Gabriel could do to bring down the wrath of a powerful immortal. "Whatever you did, I'm certain the punishment was more than you deserved."

"Hardly. I was a bit…zealous."

A flash of fangs and teeth and claws. Then it faded as quickly as it surfaced. Megan placed a hand on his arm. "Your being zealous is a good thing. You faced all those Morphs on your own. That's cause for reward, not punishment."

Amber dawned in his eyes. Gabriel picked up her hand and raised it to his mouth. His mouth pressed against her skin. The kiss was warm and lingering, as if he drew strength from her touch.

"You don't know, Megan. You can't know the half of it." Terse, flat words accompanied by the grim set of his chiseled jaw.

Gabriel cleared his throat and began a cheerful, silly Cajun song that had the twins chirping along. It was as if he'd turned into another person. Another being, hiding behind a wall of cocky amusement and charm.

His attitude did not fool her. For a few precious moments, she'd sunk inside him and seen the haunting torment blackening his spirit.

Gabriel pushed on as Megan and the twins drowsed.

A short time later, he pulled into the quiet, tree-lined drive. No gates or security needed. Tristan had no need of either.

The stately red brick mansion was as large as a hotel. White wicker chairs and tables sat on a front porch. Gabriel parked in the circular drive, shut off the engine. Hair rose on the nape of his neck. The primal need to protect his mate clawed to the surface.

Tristan was a dangerous man around a beauty

like Megan. He wasn't certain how the Guardian regarded Shadows, but he'd take no chances.

Either for seduction or capture.

The last time he'd seen the immortal, Tristan was clutching a leather whip stained with Gabriel's blood. Muscles on his back clenched in remembrance.

He gently roused the girls and Megan. When they reached the front porch, he snagged the note taped to the door.

Please come in, Gabriel. I'm out back. Make yourself at home and then bring Megan to me.

The entry hall was quiet but for the ticking of an antique grandfather clock. Wonder touched the girls' expressions as they regarded the hardwood floors, the embroidered rugs, the house's open and opulent spaces. A crystal vase of stargazer lilies adorned an oval table near the sweeping staircase. Megan broke into a pleasured smile as she examined the flowers.

"My favorites."

Honey blond hair swung past her shoulders

as she leaned down to inhale the blossoms. A small triangle of creamy skin showed where the new blouse was unbuttoned.

He steeled past the temptation to take her hand, lay her against the stairs, pull her trousers down and thrust deep inside her, staking his claim.

That would be making himself at home, all right. He smiled grimly and tipped his hat farther down on his brow.

"Such a lovely home. I've never seen anything so beautiful. This kitchen looks fit for a professional chef." Megan gave a wistful sigh.

"It should be. I designed it."

Amused, he tipped her opened jaw upward.

"You designed it, for the one who beat you?"

"And bought the house for him, as well." Gabriel examined the bottles on a custom-designed spice rack.

Seeing her expression, he shrugged. "It's complicated."

"It's a very large house."

"Filled with everything imaginable. A game room with a bowling alley, movie theater, a family room with two large screen televisions, even an outdoor tennis and basketball court."

Her pouty little mouth parted into a shocked moue. "Why?"

"It keeps him entertained." *And off my back. Literally.*

Gabriel found a cookie jar on the counter and milk in the refrigerator. He poured glasses for both girls and gave them instructions to remain in the kitchen.

"Your cousin and I need to meet with Tristan first," he told them.

Tall sliders in the kitchen opened to the lavish covered lanai.

"Why leave the girls behind?"

"Protection," he said grimly. "Tristan didn't ask to meet them. He asked only for you, *chère,* so I'm following exact instructions."

"You don't trust him."

A humorless smile touched his mouth. "Exactly."

"Then why are we here?"

Gabriel put a hand on the small of her back. "Because he's a Justice Guardian, and he's safer than Logan or Morphs. And they can't break inside."

They walked past a grouping of chairs, wet bar with widescreen television, an elegant pool with a tiled fountain, to the lush verdant lawn. A bricked pathway led to a grove of trees sheltering a shaded, small patio with comfortable chairs.

In one of the chairs Tristan sat reading. Sunlight filtered through the sugar maples and oaks, dappling the Guardian's dark hair.

He looks so ordinary, she told him. *A Phoenix wearing tan cargo shorts, a cherry-red long-sleeved sport shirt and boating shoes?*

Looks can fool, he reminded her, remembering how he'd looked the day he'd irked Tristan's ire and the Immortal had punished him.

Gabriel's chest tightened as he felt Megan's natural curiosity prick. He slid a protective arm around her waist. Immortal or not, no one was going to hurt his mate.

Tristan set down his book and had a warm smile for Megan. Gabriel didn't care for that smile or the spark of interest in the man's emerald gaze.

His mate looked wary as the Immortal stood and stretched to his full six foot five inches.

"Megan Moraine. The escaped Shadow Wolf. I've been waiting for you. You broke the law and you must pay."

No time to react. No time to panic as the Immortal lifted his long, leanly muscled arms. A scream barely escaped Megan's throat as Tristan shot her with a bolt of energy.

She pitched forward, falling to the ground as if dead.

Chapter 17

"You son-of-a..."

Gabriel caught Megan as she slumped into unconsciousness. Gently, he laid her on the bricked patio and checked her pulse. It was rapid and thready, but her breathing was even.

Primitive instinct raged. For a single moment, he lost control.

The change happened instantly. Leaping over the chair, he tackled Tristan, forgetting sense, forgetting the man could obliterate him with a single flick of a finger. Claws and fangs erupted as he snarled. Still half human, he charged, the bloodlust overtaking him.

Crimson welled on the Guardian's arm as Gabriel swiped at him. Tristan lay on his back, expression impassive as Gabriel bared his fangs.

Ready to tear out the man's throat.

Common sense took over. He pulled back the beast, suppressing his rage, sheathing his claws.

Smiling, Tristan slowly stood.

The smile dropped at the same time Gabriel delivered a powerful punch straight to his mouth. Satisfaction filled him as the Phoenix staggered back.

Caught by surprise. Bastard deserved it.

At the flash of anger crossing Tristan's expression, Gabriel steeled his spine. "Go for it. But don't you dare hurt her again or I'll tear your eyes out with my last dying breath."

Tristan wiped the blood off his mouth. The cut healed before his eyes. "Still pack a helluva punch, Gabriel. Maybe stronger than the last time you hit me. Some things never change." His gaze shot to Megan. "Well, maybe the players do."

Sickening realization shot through him. A cool, hard anger filled him as Gabriel faced the Immortal. "You set me up."

"Of course. I had to see for myself if she's the one for you."

The Phoenix went over to Megan. Gabriel bolted and blocked his path. "Stay away from her."

"Relax, Draicon. I'm just giving her a little healing jolt."

Quivering with the need to protect his mate, Gabriel forced himself to remain still as Tristan laid a hand on Megan's forehead. Lines of strain smoothed out and she yawned, sitting up. Her beautiful blue eyes blinked in confusion.

"Did I faint? I don't remember anything."

Gabriel extended a hand, helping her stand. "You were a little overcome."

"My apologies," Tristan said smoothly. "I tend to have that effect on some people when we first meet."

He encased Megan's palm in both of his, the harsh Immortal replaced by a charming man.

"Megan Moraine." Tristan brought her hand to his lips, brushed her knuckles with a brief kiss. "You are most welcome, and safe, here."

Gabriel pulled her back. Megan glanced at him and lifted her chin. "So you're a famous

Immortal who ignores the plight of my people. I'd like to say it's a pleasure to meet you, but I'd be lying."

Tristan looked surprised. "You're an escaped Shadow and you dare to confront me? Who do you think you are? I could kill you with a flick of my finger."

"Go ahead. It won't change how I feel or the truth." She took a deep breath, and he saw the effort it took to rein in her fury. "You allow others to abuse us just because we're different. And if my words offend you, tough. Yeah, you can slay me with a flick of your damn finger, but you'd be better off dealing real justice to those who deserve it, the Draicon who imprison my people and rape our females. Does the truth bother you, Phoenix? It should."

She was fading, as insubstantial as air. Filled with admiration, Gabriel slid his palm into her quivering one. Knowing her anger forced her into Shadow. Gently, he drew her to his side, murmuring soothing assurances into her mind. Gradually he felt her calm and saw her take form once more.

"You have tremendous courage. An apt mate

for a Draicon of enormous strength, and power."
Tristan gave her a long, thoughtful look.

"Gabriel has more courage and loyalty than
you ever will. You're not loyal to anyone."

"Easy, Megan." Gabriel massaged the back
of her neck and shot Tristan a vicious glare. "I
hate seeing you upset, *chère*."

Tristan cocked his head. "Megan, would you
see to the twins? I believe they've finished their
snack and they're worried about you. Your mate
and I must talk."

Only after he assured her that he'd be fine did
Megan leave. Gabriel folded his arms across his
chest. "Talk."

Frank male awareness gleamed in Tristan's
green eyes. "She's quite lovely. I've never met
a Shadow before with such passion. I'm certain
she'd be wild in bed."

Gabriel growled deep in his throat. "Touch
her, Phoenix, I'll rip your throat out."

Tristan stood silent, watching him. Then a
small smile curved his mouth upward, a sensual
mouth that had kissed thousands of women into
sexual submission over the centuries.

"Perhaps I shall."

Gabriel lunged forward. He fell on the Immortal with a ferocious snarl. Everything inside him that was the primitive beast howled. *Mine, mine!*

Then fell back by a bolt of sheer electricity driven into his carotid. Stunned, he lay on the warm brick. His mind raged to protect Megan, to defend her from the uncaring sensual being that would take her without tenderness, without regard and toss her aside like refuse.

"You care."

A statement from the Phoenix. Calm, assessing.

Gabriel struggled to stand. "I will go down fighting to protect someone as beautiful and courageous as her from you."

He fisted his hands. Wolf raged to the surface. He didn't fight it, but welcomed the animal inside that would die to protect her, to keep her safe and happy....

Happy?

"The two have become one. Your wolf has bonded, my friend."

Gabriel stood back, his fists uncurling, the fingers long and elegant as he stared at them.

A Feral wolf didn't care about personal happiness. A Feral wolf only cared about protecting his turf, defending that which he defined as his own.

"A very human emotion." Tristan stepped back. "Go to her, Gabriel. Seal your bond in the flesh, a bond of the heart and the soul. Bring her to ecstasy and the mating lock. It is time."

"I can't bear for her to become what I am." Gabriel looked away, shuttering his thoughts so the Immortal could not see inside him.

"How can she make the decision for herself, when she knows not what you truly are?"

"Who the hell are you to tell me what to do?"

Tristan put his hand on Gabriel's shoulder. "The Guardian of your humanity, my friend."

"I'm far from human."

"You are more human than you realize."

Stubborn pride filled him. He would not capitulate to the Phoenix's suggestions.

"A demand, not a suggestion."

Gabriel stiffened and told Tristan to go do something to himself in Cajun French.

The Guardian looked amused. "Now that is

beyond even my powers. Do as I say, Gabriel. Tell Megan what you really are or lose her."

Going preternaturally still, he searched the other man's face. "What are you threatening?"

He knew his tricks, knew the Immortal's clever manipulations.

"I never threaten. I only act. If you don't tell Megan, then she's free to leave you and seek other male company. I'll make her free of the bond that seals you together."

Stunned, he stared. "You can't do that." No one, not even a powerful Immortal, could break the destined bond of two Draicon.

"I can," Tristan said calmly. "Megan will be able to move on and have children with any male. In addition to setting her people free, she nurtures a secret dream of having a home and a family of her own."

Gabriel did, as well, but feared what kind of child he'd produce. The Phoenix watched him without emotion.

"The choice is yours, Gabriel. Now, go to her. I'll see to the twins and give you time alone. Alex's girls are intelligent and need to feel secure and safe. I want to assess their aptitude and education."

The Immortal turned and left. For a long while afterward, Gabriel remained alone.

Screams of laughter echoed outside. Gabriel lifted a lace curtain with the back of his hand as he and Megan stared down from their second-story bedroom.

In the pool, the twins played water volleyball with Tristan. The Immortal appeared relaxed and unthreatening.

"He won't hurt them," Gabriel assured Megan, reading her mind. "Tristan does keep his word."

"He hurt you when you were younger."

"I deserved it."

As they left the window, Megan slipped her hand into his. "How can a young Draicon deserve something that severe? I felt what he could do."

Gabriel ground to a halt. "You couldn't remember."

"I pretended. I didn't want him having the advantage, not when you were tense because of what happened." She tried to touch her mind to his, assure him that she was on his side. "I'm with you, Gabriel."

Their bedroom had a king-size four-poster bed. Gabriel sat, patting a space besides him.

Instinct urged her to touch, to explore, to bond with him. Megan slid a hand over his muscular thigh, feeling the hard muscle clench beneath her gentle strokes. "Why did Tristan beat you, Gabriel?"

Sighing, he tossed his hat onto a white ottoman. "I bit him. So he whipped me."

An amused look came over him as he regarded her expression. Gabriel touched her mouth with the tip of one finger.

"Were you brave or just insane?"

"Both. I was wild back then, unable to control myself."

She sensed more than saw the shame accompanying the confession.

"I'm sure he deserved it. He doesn't seem a very fair person. I wish I had bit him."

Gabriel picked up her hand, kissing her knuckles. "I'm glad you didn't, and I deserved it."

"How young were you when you confronted him?"

"Ten." He gave a bitter laugh at her shock. "I told you, I was much wilder when I was young."

"I can't imagine you being so savage that you'd bite an Immortal."

"Can you imagine me as a Feral wolf?"

"At age ten? Draicon don't shift that early."

"Trans-Ferals do."

Her palms suddenly went cold and clammy. Megan yanked her trembling hand away as her heart lodged in her throat. Her head spun with this terrifying revelation.

"You can't be." She swallowed hard. "They're extinct."

He hesitated and she saw a flash of anguish in his dark gaze. "Most of us were killed off long ago. The gene is very rare, but surfaces in my family tree once every seven generations or so. I drew the lucky card." A bitter laugh followed. "You're not a freak, Megan. I am. A fanged, wild freak who is feared by his own people. They say my kind is a hybrid wolf, human and demon."

Afraid if she said anything he'd stop, she focused on his face, his eyes now glowing amber. *Trans-Feral.* Killer wolves who hunted and tore apart anyone they wished, who were more animal than Draicon. Terror crept down her spine on spidery legs. Megan felt herself begin to fade into Shadow. His expression shuttered.

But deep inside, she pushed past the fight or fade instinct. Gabriel had finally opened up to her. Gaining his trust was more important than superstitious fears.

She assumed her form once more. "I'm sorry, Gabriel. I didn't mean to do that. Go on. I'm listening."

Gabriel retrieved his hat, slid it on his head and tipped it down. He paced the expansive room and his boot heels made a rhythmic clicking on the hardwood floor.

"I manifested my abilities fairly early." His full mouth twitched. "My parents took Alex and Etienne, my older brothers, away for the summer. They left me with relatives in northern Louisiana because they were afraid I couldn't control myself around the humans." Gabriel gave a derisive snort. "As if I'd eat them. My aunt and uncle knew I was a Trans-Feral. Their way of dealing with it was to lock me inside a steel cage.

"I went a little *fou,* crazy, while caged. I nearly clawed my cousin when he came by just to talk. He felt sorry for me. Toward the end of the two months, Tristan arrived at the request of my uncle. He unlocked the cage and I thought I was free."

Gabriel drew in a loud breath. "He taunted me, Megan. Told me I was a freak. Said if I didn't stop acting like a damn animal, I was going back into the cage permanently on display for humans to stare at. I reacted."

"You bit him."

"More." He turned, the lower half of his face shrouded in regret. "The thought of being caged again sent me over the edge. I went Feral and aimed for his throat."

Images flashed in her mind: blood pouring over Tristan's splayed fingers, the Immortal gasping. The horrified looks of Gabriel's uncle, aunt and cousins.

"He can't die, but he felt the pain and it was damn uncomfortable. The test proved I lacked discipline over my animal half. So he beat me. Taught me a lesson I'd never forget. Said he'd send me to a prison with demons for company."

Gabriel tipped up his hat, his solemn gaze meeting hers. "He spent five days teaching me to put a lid on my emotions. Tristan had me stay in human form and get out my rage and fear by beating on a junk car with a sledgehammer. He told me if I ever wanted to go Feral to hurt anyone other than my enemies, to think of the car and how badly damaged it was. That's what I could do to an innocent. He gave me hope I could be better than I was, could learn self-control. Then he promised me that if I ever needed it, I could call in a favor. Said he'd keep my secret about being a Trans-Feral and he'd offer refuge at a time in my life when I needed it most."

"You used that favor for us. When you could have used it for yourself."

He gave a half shrug of those wide shoulders.

But something in his dark expression warned her there was more. "Staying here wasn't the favor, was it?"

"I made him promise to keep you and the twins away from Enforcers. No Enforcer will turn you in, Megan. You're safe and so are the girls."

Her heart turned over at his immense loyalty. She dreaded the answer. "What did you have to promise in return, Gabriel?"

"No reason to worry, *chère*. It'll never come to pass."

He came to the bed, sat and tossed his hat aside. Gabriel gathered her hands into his, stroking his thumbs over her palms. "*Je connais pas quel*...there I go again, speaking French."

A wry smile tugged his mouth. "I don't know what the future holds, Megan. You know what I am. I'm a beast. I've tried to control it, learned discipline. But sometimes, it gets the best of me. I learned when I was little that I've always been different, and even Draicon close to you don't like different."

She slipped into his mind. Hurt and confusion filling the little boy's dark eyes as he sat on the front porch steps. His parents driving away in a carriage with his brothers, laughing while Gabriel was left behind.

Why not me, Papa?

Megan pulled away. She swallowed hard past the tears burning her throat. She mustn't show pity.

"Did I ever tell you about the tiger I invented

when I was young? Before my island became a prison?" she asked.

Gabriel shook his head.

"There were no other Shadows my age. The Draicon children visiting on the island, they made fun of me. I had no friends, so I invented this invisible tiger. I taught him to swim, because there were lots of lovely fish to catch.

"Of course when I put the fish into the bedroom of the woman whose house I cleaned in exchange for rent for Gram and myself, I blamed the tiger. After all, he was invisible."

"Did you get into trouble?"

Megan shook her head. "I told her it was Tiger's fault and he did it because she made me scrub the floor every day. The woman was a little scared, thinking a live, invisible tiger was prowling in her house. So I didn't have to scrub the floor every day. Just every other day."

He laughed. "Good for you."

"See, there are advantages to being different."

Gabriel gave a small smile. "Thank you, *chère*." His deep, quiet voice was filled with sincerity. He tweaked her nose. "For making me laugh again."

He picked up her hands and turned them over. "Such strong yet delicate hands. Working so hard since you were a small girl. No playmates but a tiger."

Emotions warred inside her. "I was so alone, Gabriel. I tried to act tough, as if it didn't matter. The other kids didn't like me because I could turn invisible."

"Like me." He kissed her fingers, one by one. "Except other kids wouldn't play with me because they sensed I was too dangerous."

Intensity radiated in his dark gaze. "I won't ever go Feral on you, Megan. It's too dangerous. Trust me, *chère.* It's why I chose not to shift into wolf back at the service plaza."

His kiss was tender, gentle.

But she wanted more. Sensing his savage hunger, she whispered to him. "Don't hold back on me, Gabriel. I can take what you want to give."

The thud of boots falling to the hard floor, the rasp of his zipper sliding downward… Megan removed her own clothing with trembling hands.

His hands stroked over her skin slowly, with

tenderness and possession. Her heightened senses took in the warmth of his skin, the masculine scent of him, the salty taste of his skin beneath her tongue as she licked his collarbone.

The deep timbre of his voice echoed in her ear. He slid a hand down her thigh then rolled over.

"Ride me, my little Shadow. Show me you aren't afraid of us achieving a mating lock and you receiving my powers."

Desire was a harsh whip across her sensitive skin. Megan slid down on his throbbing erection. A low groan tore from his throat as she sheathed him. Bracing her hands on his muscular chest, she began to move. Slowly. Each exquisite motion wrung another emotion from him. Red flashed in his eyes. The beast.

She gave a small, sexy pout to mask the tiny anxiety. The mating lock would turn her into something as dark, dangerous as his beast.

Shuttering the thought, she concentrated on teasing her wolf. Drawing pleasure from each slow rise and fall of her hips. Gabriel wrapped his hands around her waist, pushing her upward. He let her have control.

For a few minutes more.

Then in an apt move, he flipped her over, spread her legs open wide and slammed into her. Each slap of his flesh against hers heightened the pleasure. He trailed his mouth over her neck, lightly licked her earlobe.

She moved against him, snarling in return as she tasted his salty skin. Gabriel never stopped his heavy thrusts as she nipped and marked him.

He leaned over, nuzzling her neck, and bit her on the sensitive juncture of her neck. She threw back her head and whimpered with pleasure. Wrapping her legs around him, she met his heavy thrusts as they tangled together. Megan screamed his name as she climaxed, followed by his hoarse shout.

When they collapsed back onto the bed, she kept a single thought guarded from him.

She wasn't afraid of the mating lock making them one, giving her his Feral powers.

She was terrified.

Chapter 18

Lying naked in bed, Megan snatched at the strawberry Gabriel dangled before her nose. He chuckled as he jerked it out of reach. The sheets tangled around his lean hips, he rested against the carved headboard. His dark, ragged hair was tousled after their savage bout of lovemaking. A bite mark on the strong muscles of his neck was evidence of her possession.

She stopped reaching for the strawberry, a different hunger pulling as she studied his long, lean torso. Wicked knowing gleamed in his gaze.

Gabriel dipped the strawberry in chocolate. A droplet fell onto her breast. Slowly, he licked it off. She shivered with pleasure.

"Let me see your tongue, and I'll reward you," he promised.

Instead, she sat up and gave a sultry smile. Megan slid her hands along his chest, toyed with the flat brown circles of his nipples. Hard muscle lined his flat belly. Then she boldly yanked down the sheet. Hair marched from his deep chest to the indentation of his belly button, dipping into a line that ended with the thicker, black hair on his groin. His body was wiry, but well-sculpted. He radiated strength and danger.

His penis lay against his muscular thigh, twitching as if it sensed her intent.

"Maybe I'm tired of strawberries."

Megan bent her head and slid her hands around his arousal. She began to stroke and then dipped her finger into the chocolate, smearing it on the head.

Her mouth encased him. Megan swirled and sucked. Passion and feelings guided her past her inexperience.

Judging from the low groans, she wasn't doing too badly.

Beneath her, his body tightened. Gabriel

fisted his hands in her hair and pulled her up-right.

"Enough," he gasped. "You will be the death of me, *ma petite chou.*"

He rolled her onto her stomach, nudged her legs apart with a knee. His firm palms settled on her hips. In this position she felt exposed and vulnerable and oddly free.

It was the traditional mating position for Draicon, she realized. The submissive female, leading the male to tangle in rough, wild sex.

"Lift your hips," he commanded.

She braced herself on her hands, wriggled her bottom at him in a come-hither invitation.

I'm ready for this.

With that single thought, he made a sound low in his throat and pushed deep inside her. Megan gasped as his thick cock slid into her swollen, sensitive tissues. Gabriel gripped her hips and rocked against her. Each thrust made her claw the sheets. His deep groans of pleasure threaded with her excited cries.

They came together, in blinding, shattering pleasure.

After, she rested her head against his deep

chest, listening to the reassuring beat of his heart. He stroked her hair, rubbing the strands between his thumb and forefinger.

"How could your family be frightened of you? I could never be frightened of you." She snuggled against him.

He went still, his deep voice ominous. "Don't be so certain, *ma petite chou*. Life has a way of delivering unexpected, cruel surprises when we make such bold assertions."

Idly she stroked over the inked mark on his muscled bicep. "What is this?"

Gabriel stiffened. "My heritage."

He rolled out of bed and stood, giving a luxurious stretch. Hugging her knees, Megan sat up. Thick muscle corded his long, lean body. She had known every pleasure of that body as it plunged into hers over and over.

Her hungry gaze roved over the bulging biceps, the hard stomach and the long, thick length of his penis dangling between his legs. Gabriel caught her staring.

What an animal.

Megan sensed him catching her thought, like a child's palm encasing a floating dandelion fluff. She saw him flinch and felt a forlorn sense of sorrow.

In bed, she added.

A wicked smile replaced the wary look. She thought of how wild and untamed he'd been and the passion they'd shared. Suddenly her lower belly grew taut with yearning and heat suffused her entire body. Sweet pressure built between her legs as if someone were licking…

There. She bit back a low moan as the pressure intensified. He was toying with her mind, wickedly making her brain imagine his mouth was…

A scream fled her as she climaxed. Megan collapsed against the pillows, her body trembling from the sensual onslaught.

"How, you…" She felt dazed and well-loved. "You're a bad boy."

"A good bad boy." Gabriel grinned, ran a hand through his hair. "My Megan."

His voice was deep and sexy. The kiss he dropped on her cheek was tame, but the look in his amber eyes was not. "My wild little beast."

For a moment, he remained on the bed, quietly stroking her hair. Peace settled over his face. He looked happy. Her heart did a little jump. She was falling for him, hard and fast. And finally, he'd shared himself and there was hope that maybe, just maybe, he would keep doing so.

From his being inside her mind, all his guards dropped. Megan felt his intimate thoughts, and shock pummeled through her. She drew back.

"Gabriel, you weren't telling me the truth because you wanted to. You told me you're a Trans-Feral because Tristan threatened you."

His chocolate gaze went hard and flat as he withdrew his hand. "Yes."

Gabriel hadn't chosen to share himself with her. He'd been forced into it. Disappointment surged through her.

"I thought you wanted to be close with me." She bit her lip. "All of me, not just the physical closeness. And you were holding back all this time. Why, Gabriel? Why couldn't you tell me the whole truth?"

A muscle ticked in his hard jaw. "Megan, I never meant to hurt your feelings. But it's your turn for the truth now. Had I told you about my Trans-Feral nature earlier, would you have

stayed? Or turned and run with the twins because you were too scared?"

His mouth a thin slash, he placed a hand on
her neck as he sat on the bed. Warm breath
feathered over her cheek as he whispered hotly
into her ear.

"Would you truly like, *chère,* to see what I
am? How dangerous my kind are? How we can
kill without thought?" Gabriel took her earlobe
between his teeth and nipped gently.

She thought of how he'd dispatched the
Morphs, as easily as dusting off his hands.

"I don't know. Honestly. I probably would
have been scared." Pulse racing, she studied her
lover. "But you said before that you wouldn't
hurt me. I have trust in that, Gabriel, more than
I have in the brick fortress you put up around
yourself so you can keep me out. You think to
hide yourself from me, like I hide in Shadow.
You're not a violent person. You do whatever
you must to protect and defend your own. In
that way, you're as transparent as glass."

"Glass can shatter, and injure people. That's
what I do."

A steel barrier closed around his mind as rigid

as the hurricane shutters he'd used to protect his cottage. Gabriel pulled away.

A heartbeat of silence. "Do you share all of yourself with me, Megan? Everything?"

Memories flashed; the red-eyed beast stalking her dreams. "Everything important."

"And yet you won't tell me of your nightmares."

Shame mingled with old terrors. "It's complicated."

"I see." He slid out of bed, pulled on his jeans. "I need to check on the girls."

Something inside her snapped. "Don't shut me out. I'm tired of living in Shadow and everyone treating me as if I'm invisible even when I'm not."

Megan stood, feeling vulnerable in her nudity, but refusing to cover herself. Her voice dropped to a raw whisper. "My nightmares aren't important. What is important is where I stand with you, and knowing you trust me enough to share yourself. Why can't you open to me, Gabriel? I'd never betray you."

The black felt cowboy hat he slid on blocked his eyes, his soul, from her view. Megan did not say anything, but waited. Please, she thought with her whole heart.

Then he turned away, thumbs hooked through the belt loops of his faded jeans. "Don't ask this of me, Megan. I can't."

Her opened arms fell to her sides like lead weights. Megan took one physical step back, and ten emotional steps. "Go check on the girls. I'll be down soon."

When he left, she fisted her hands to hold the tears in check. Mustn't let anyone know. Tristan and the girls would not suspect the bleak truth.

Gabriel was more of a Shadow than she ever would become.

She dressed, her movements slow and mechanical. Then suddenly she felt something warm and wet trickle down her cool cheek.

Megan flung herself facedown on the soft bed. She cried for the loss of a long-held dream.

For Gabriel, who could not turn to her in trust, and tell her what he felt deep inside.

She was alone.

More than she'd ever felt on the island. A Draicon Shadow with a bonded mate.

The door creaked open and Gabriel stepped

inside. Hastily she wiped away the last of her tears. Pride made her greet him as if nothing were wrong.

Hands jammed into his pockets, he strode forward. His skin was stretched tight over taut cheekbones.

"I hate to see you so upset. It kills me inside."

Sitting beside her, Gabriel kissed the corner of her mouth and drew her into his arms. Megan parted her lips beneath the insistent pressure of his, sighing as his tongue swept into her mouth. Then she yanked back, holding out her hands like a stop sign.

"This isn't the answer, Gabriel. I want all of you. I've been alone so long, dreaming of the one who could set me free. Someone who would accept me for everything I am, and would let me inside his world, as well."

Her voice trembled. "I've wanted to give you my trust and my hope. But you keep shoving me away, just like they did on the island, only they did it out of ignorance and fear."

His thumbs gently wiped away the tears spilling out of the corners of her eyes. "I want to start over again. Begin a new life, with you. I can't promise anything but to try."

"It's all I ask, Gabriel."

He tipped up her chin so she could look him straight in the eye. "You deserve everything good to come your way. I've never met a female more kindhearted or strong. You will be free, Megan. No more hiding in the shadows."

She dared to press further. "Why didn't you trust me before to tell me about what you really are?"

"This isn't easy. I want you to trust me, Megan, and believe in me, so I'll take the gamble." He removed his hat. "I didn't want to tell you about my being a Trans-Feral before because I was afraid."

"Afraid of trusting me with the knowledge?"

"Afraid of your reaction. Anyone who knows what I am has never reacted…ah, favorably." A twisted grin touched his mouth. "More like they act as if I'm Hell's spawn come to earth. I didn't want to see it in your face, see what I've seen in others."

"What is it, Gabriel?" She kept her voice low and soothing.

"Damn this is hard." He scrubbed a hand over the bristles on his jaw. Gabriel sat down. The honest plea in his dark gaze floored her. "I just, I want…"

"Tell me," she urged.

"Can you promise me that you will trust me utterly? With your life if I should ever change and become fully Trans-Feral?"

"I trust you."

"Promise, Megan. Promise me you won't call me a monster." His voice dropped. "I don't think I could bear it, knowing my bonded mate thought I was one when all my life I've tried to convince myself I'm not."

She seized his hands into hers. "I promise."

"I didn't tell you before because I was afraid of your reaction. Afraid you'd act like someone else had."

The pain radiating from him was so intense, she felt an actual ache in her chest. Megan laced her fingers through his. "Please, tell me, Gabriel."

But he couldn't look her in the eye. "I'll show you instead. Close your eyes."

As she did, a series of images unfolded in her

mind: a tall, voluptuous brunette, laughing and walking with Gabriel. Megan felt his absolute adoration, heard his thoughts. He was nineteen and Tamara was the one. Everything pointed to it, even though she was his first lover.

The chemistry was right, the sex amazing. He was certain he'd found his destined mate. Nothing could go wrong.

Everything had.

A Morph attacked her. By the time Gabriel reached her, he was crazy with fear and Tamara was successfully fighting off the Morph. But infuriated and needing to prove his manhood, he shifted.

"Your eyes, oh Gabriel, what's happening with your eyes?!" Tamara screamed.

Now Megan saw through Gabriel's eyes, felt his rage and his fear for his lover as he became Trans-Feral. And then after he'd killed the Morph, his love backed away with horror in her eyes, throwing out her hands.

"Stay away from me, you monster!" Tamara shouted.

Megan's heart sank as she watched a lonely Gabriel walk away in human form. Tamara screaming about telling her parents about the dangerous Trans-Feral, and how he should be locked away in a demon prison.

A saddened Gabriel forced to erase all memories of himself and their relationship from Tamara's mind.

Megan's eyes opened to see Gabriel quietly regarding her. She took his face into her hands and kissed him tenderly. "I'm so sorry," she breathed against his mouth. "If I could, I'd erase your past. How could she do such a thing when you were only protecting her?"

Gabriel ran a finger down her cheek. "Fear. Tamara didn't know what I was. I never warned her. But now you know. Don't ever be afraid of me, Megan. I'd never hurt you, no matter what I was. It's bred into my blood and bones to protect you to my dying breath."

"I'd trust in that even if you shifted into a Trans-Feral."

He gave a sad smile. "I hope so. I hope it never comes down to that."

Chapter 19

Gabriel focused on the busy stretch of I-10 into New Orleans as Megan and the girls dozed off. Tristan had given them a sleek new minivan. They looked like a typical American family on a road trip. The drive had been long and silent but for the incessant, excited chatter of the twins as they anticipated seeing their father. Tristan had been impressed by both girls.

"They're extremely smart, disciplined and show a ready aptitude to learn, despite the restrictions they've lived under on Shadow Island," Tristan had told Gabriel and Megan. He aimed a thoughtful look at Megan. "Someone has taught them well."

Megan had said nothing, only curled her hand into Gabriel's.

Beside him, she awoke with a small cry. Sweat dampened her forehead. He reached over, gave her hand a reassuring squeeze. "The same dream?"

Trembling, she nodded. He brought her hand to his lips, kissed it gently. "Tell me, darling."

"I can't," she said, pushing at her hair. "It will feed its power over me."

Then she said nothing else.

Taking a leap of faith, he opened his mind to her. He touched her chest and her heavily beating heart. "When you hurt here, I hurt, as well. You will always be part of me."

Megan took his palm and placed it against her cheek. She turned into his touch, her long silky lashes feathering against her soft cheeks.

"You're so good to me, Gabriel. I'm glad we're destined to be together."

A rush of emotions left him staring wordlessly at her. Gabriel marveled at finally finding a woman who didn't treat him like a pariah.

"When Alex comes, I want you to go with him and my brothers. It's safer at my parents' house." He grimaced. "Until Logan and I have it out, you're not safe."

Logan was near. Every sense screamed it.

They passed the Super Dome, Gabriel exited the interstate, heading for Basin Street.

"Keep your guard up," he warned. "Alex said he'd meet us at the cemetery."

"An odd choice. Why not your restaurant or your home? Or his?"

"Too obvious. Alex said he shielded the place against Morphs, so it's safe. None of Logan's Morph clones can make it inside."

"Nothing can tear down the shield?"

"Certain types of demons can, but there haven't been any in these parts in decades. Tristan and the other Guardians trapped them."

"Uncle Gabriel, you didn't tell our daddy who we were yet, did you?" Jennifer asked.

"We want to surprise him," added Jillian.

"Ah, he'll be surprised, all right," he assured them.

Wide-eyed, the girls quieted as he drove toward the St. Louis Cemetery Number One. Gabriel parked the car on the street.

He looked around. Hairs stood up at the nape of his neck, yet he could scent no danger. Yet.

"Maybe it's just being here, at a cemetery."

Megan's voice broke through his introspection. For the first time, he realized he'd allowed her inside him, to experience his thoughts and emotions. It wasn't as invasive as he'd envisioned. Or as intimidating. Rather, he felt her presence as gentle and reassuring.

I'm with you, all the way. We have to think of the girls, and Alexandre. It's going to be a little scary for the twins and for him, as well.

He squeezed her palm. A small smile touched her mouth. Gabriel rolled his shoulders to ease the tension, watchful as they climbed out of the car.

Humidity hung in the air like a wet blanket. He breathed in the familiar smells: alcohol from Bourbon Street, magnolias and dank earth, river water, diesel fuel from the Mississippi, garbage, fried crayfish, a thousand scents of humans and other creatures, and the reassuring, earthy scent of Draicon wolves.

Megan's own nostrils pricked. Surprise stole over her expression. "I smell…is that a vampire?"

He tweaked her pert nose. "Darling, you are in New Orleans. Don't be surprised to see a Fae or two, as well. Heard there's a convention in town."

Blond dolls dangling from their tight grips, Jillian and Jennifer stared at the scrolling iron-work cross over the cemetery gate. "I've never been to a place like this before. It has the aura of magick," Jennifer whispered.

Using his powers, he unlocked the gate. "Let me check it out first, then I'll come and get you."

After combing through the graveyard, he returned. They wended their way through the lanes of brick, marble and stone tombs. The air was hot and sultry, licking their skin with heat. Gabriel remained edgy and alert for trouble. But he scented only the humans who'd walked through here during tours and heard only the stillness of a slight breeze whispering through the graveyard.

Yet he couldn't shake the feeling something was off. Beneath the normal smells of the city lurked a foul scent, like sulfur and methane.

His nostrils flared.

"Spooky place." Megan had her arms around the twins.

He glanced at the hazy outline of the yellow afternoon sun. "We're still early."

The girls wandered off to examine the writings on a tomb. Keeping an eye on them, Gabriel ran a finger down Megan's cheek.

"They'll be with their father soon."

Gabriel felt the tension in her body ratchet up. "I know how cruel Draicon can be." She bit her lower lip. "All the verbal and physical abuse Normals dished out because I was a Shadow, I've fought my whole life to convince myself I'm not lower than dirt. I did the same for Jenny and Jilly. For every insult a Normal gave them, I told them how special they are and made them feel they were worth something."

In a flash of clarity, he understood. "You're worried you're handing them over to someone who will make them feel bad about themselves."

Megan nodded. "Draicon made my life hell. Why should I trust their father, any Draicon, can be good to Shadows? I guess I was hoping deep down that their father would be a Shadow."

"I know how deeply Alex loved Simone and

Amelia and how respectful he is of Shadows. He'll love the girls with all his heart. This will give life back to my brother. He's been walking in a fog ever since they died."

"I believe you. You're loyal and protective and courageous to the core. And yet you hide from the world, because you don't want the world to truly see you. If they saw you as I do, they'd know exactly how wonderful you are."

He gave a brief smile. "Not so wonderful when I show my dark side."

"I don't care," she said fiercely. "Nothing you could turn into would make me turn away from you, Gabriel."

Such easy acceptance.

Suddenly a stench made him gag. He leaned back, coughing. Everything inside him flared to high alert.

Something nasty and sinister lurked in the shadows.

"What is it?"

"I don't know, but stick close," he warned.

Movement caught the corner of his eye. Megan dodged a blow, the bat missing her by a fraction of an inch. Gabriel went to push her behind him, but she dropped and rolled away.

An unearthly screech echoed over the cemetery. Gabriel stiffened. His subconscious recognized the intruder.

"What was that?" Megan cried out.

"A demon. Protect the girls." He tensed, waiting to attack. Not knowing where the ability came from, but going on a long-buried instinct.

Alex had shielded the cemetery against Morphs, but not against demons. They were screwed.

The dark cloud materialized and the girls cried out as they were seized.

Clad in a torn white shirt and ragged pants, the man gripped a twin by each wrist. He flashed a cruel smile at Gabriel.

"I smell a filthy dog who needs to be put down, along with his brother's hellish spawn."

A voice with a distinct Southern twang, once friendly and trustworthy. Sickened, he regarded his former employee. He'd known Jay for ten years, had taken him into his inner circle. The human was loyal to the core. Until now.

Jay was the reason the Shadow Friends network was compromised, he realized.

He circled closer, getting his bearings, using his sharpened senses to track the man's moves. "How did you find me?"

Jay laughed. "You're so cocky, Gabriel. All I had to do was plant a tracking device on the one item you're never without. *Le chapeau.*"

The thick air of malice felt smothering. Gabriel tore off his hat, examined the band and pulled free a miniature chip. He crushed the GPS, threw the hat aside.

"I've made you rich, Jay. Why the betrayal?"

"Logan promised the entire chain of your restaurants would be mine when you died. All I had to do was give him the locations of the safe houses."

Gabriel drew in a lungful of foul air. The inner voice nudged him to the warning signs, the foul breath, the wild-eyed reddish glare, the trembling of limbs no longer under his control. Anguish tore through him.

Jay was no longer human.

Gabriel tamped down his fury and grief. He couldn't push it and unleash his wolf with the girls at risk. Deep inside, his friend still remained, trapped and screaming for release from the prison of his own body.

In a moment of blinding empathy, Gabriel felt pity for his friend's panicked helplessness. He told Megan. *Run, get out of here.*

She threw him a distraught look. *Not while he has the girls.*

Megan whirled as movement stirred the air. Logan darted out from between two tombstones. He slammed Megan against a wrought iron fence. She recovered and delivered a blow that sent the Draicon reeling. Gabriel was torn between protecting his draicara, who was fighting well on her own, and dealing with the immediate threat to the twins.

I'm fine, I can handle this coullion. *Take care of the girls.*

"Jenny, Jilly, use all your powers," Gabriel ordered.

Jennifer released her doll, sending it floating above Jay's head, distracting him. Then Jennifer shoved him backward while Jillian's brow furrowed in concentration.

Jay screamed. "Get out of my head! Out!"

The twins yanked free and fled.

Gabriel delivered a hard punch to the man's solar plexus. Jay doubled over, gasping, then recovered. He flashed Gabriel a sickly grin.

"I'm ten times stronger now than I was as a puny human." Jay dodged as Gabriel lashed out.

For every blow Gabriel delivered, the man recovered with amazing speed. And then for a split instant, Jay lifted his gaze. Gone was the reddish glare, replaced by hazel eyes filled with anguish.

"I'm dead, Gabe," Jay whispered. "Kill me. It's the only way I'll have peace."

He couldn't. This was the man who had stood by his side, helped him establish the Shadow network, the guy who'd drank beers with him in the late hours after they'd closed the restaurant. Jay was more than a loyal employee. He was a close friend and Gabriel had once trusted him with his life.

But everything Feral inside him raged, knowing Jay spoke the truth.

And then the demon did something that made Jay scream in pain. Rage consumed Gabriel. He snarled, feeling his savage side take over. "I'm sorry, Jay."

With a howl that echoed through the lonely cemetery, he grabbed his former manager, lifting him as Jay fought and yelled in demon speak.

Muscles strained to control the demon. With a loud curse, Gabriel impaled him on the pointed spikes of an ornate tomb fence. For a moment peace came across his old friend's features.

A foul whoosh of air pushed past Gabriel. Without thought, he whirled and snarled, talons exploding from his fingertips and raking over the dark cloud.

The demon's scream echoed in his mind as he saw the black mass explode into small shards of inky darkness.

He turned to the sound of frightened screams.

The twins tried to shift into Shadow as Logan threw a silver net over them. The girls writhed against the bonds. The sharp netting cut her hands as Megan tried to free her cousins.

Then she too was trapped by another net. The burning stench of fear filled Gabriel's nostrils as she fought the bonds.

Horror shone in her eyes. Each movement against the net weakened her powers. Logan fished out a knife and turned to Gabriel.

"You're a Morph now. The shield should keep you out." Gabriel fisted his hands, advancing, watching the other's moves.

"Hitchhiker demons can eradicate a puny Draicon shield. Don't you know anything, Feral?" The man blinked, showing coal in the pits of his eyes. "I gave up everything to avenge my son's death. My money. My business. My soul. I turned Morph by killing my brother as a blood sacrifice for the demon and made an army of Morph clones to come after you. Now your loved ones will suffer like you made my Deke suffer, you Feral bastard. I'm going to cut them to pieces, slowly."

Rage consumed Gabriel. The howl he released echoed through the stillness of the cemetery. Savage. Inhuman. The wild animal inside him wanted the blood of the man who threatened his loved ones.

Logan stepped closer to the net, drew his knife over Megan's right cheek. Blood welled.

Maddened by the sight, Gabriel felt fury

shape his cells, twist his bones. Without warning, he shifted into what everyone feared.

Ignoring the dangers, knowing he must protect his own, he allowed the bloodlust to surface.

A monster emerged before her shocked gaze.

Gabriel's eyes turned black like a Morph's. An instant later, he blinked and they were red as blood. An inhuman growl rumbled from his throat. Bones lengthened and limbs widened.

His jaw elongated like a wolf's and yet he didn't transform into wolf. Instead, his angular face became sharpened, his nose pointed like a knife blade. He opened his mouth to reveal pointed, razor sharp teeth.

Talons erupted from his fingertips. Dark gray fur sprouted along his muscular forearms. The jeans he wore split at the seams as muscle and bone shifted. Then his clothing vanished. Fur rippled along his spine, his flat stomach, his groin. Yet he did not shift into wolf, but remained standing, hunched over.

A creature of darkness.

And he was the darkness, the raw wild, the

Feral, living only to breathe and hunt and exist as pure killer wolf. Man was buried deep, far beneath.

The creature roared and with a powerful punch, sent Logan hurling against the wrought iron fence. Then it sprang forward and tore open the netting trapping her and the twins. The silver didn't diminish its powers.

Megan grabbed the girls' hands and raced to safety, pushing them behind her as she watched the battle.

The beast roared again. Blood sprayed over ancient tombstones as it clawed at Logan's throat. It was over very quickly. The beast snarled at what was left of Logan's body.

It looked up, its blood red gaze meeting hers, and then it gave a low growl.

She shrank back as the thunder of boots pounded into the lane. Megan's frightened gaze swept over four tall Draicon males, one dressed in black leather and bearing close resemblance to Gabriel.

His brothers. She knew them from his description. Etienne, the oldest, next in line to lead their pack. Damian, the adopted brother who led his own pack in New Mexico. Raphael, the Draicon Kallan, an Immortal with the power to end the life of a Draicon. And Alexandre with his sharp blue eyes and short graying hair. The girls' father.

The creature stood silently watching them.

Alexandre came forward, holding out his hand. He was slightly shorter than the others, and his lean body had an air of whipcord toughness. "Gabe? Hey, man, it's us, your brothers. It's Alex. C'mon, calm down. It's okay." He glanced at Megan. "This is Megan, your bonded mate? You're scaring her. Shift back."

A flash of iridescent sparks, as if Gabriel struggled to recover. But the monster remained standing.

It looked to her, licking its sharp canines as if she were a tasty treat, and advanced. The creature held out a bloodied hand. A deep voice sounded inside her head. *Megan, I can't shift back. Help me. Come to me, I need you.*

The monster from her nightmares stood before her. A scream died in her throat as old terrors surfaced of blood spurting and flesh tearing.

"Get away from me," she shrieked. Instinctively she faded into Shadow. Megan ran toward the twins, shielding them with her arms.

"Jenny, Jilly, come with me. Back away slowly, or it might hurt you."

The creature attempted to smile with its wet, reddened mouth. "Trust me, Megan," it said in a grating, deep voice. "I would never hurt you."

Words from her darkest nightmare. It was coming true. She could almost feel the burning pain from the sharp talons raking over her throat. Megan glanced down at the remains of Logan's dismembered body.

Drooling, the Feral werewolf advanced. She tried to remember it was Gabriel, the man who'd made such passionate love to her. Her courage surged and she forced herself to take form again. To reveal herself as he had.

But the fangs, talons and blood terrified her. How could this thing from her darkest dreams be Gabriel? As the creature reached out a hand to her, Megan stepped back with a sob.

"Don't come any closer," she warned.

Please, Megan, it's Gabriel, your mate. Don't run from me. I need you.

This creature couldn't be her beloved Gabriel. It was the walking, talking beast from her nightmare, come to take her back to Shadow Island and torture her.

"Don't touch me."

The creature's hand dropped and it looked away, as if ashamed to meet her gaze.

"Cousin Megan?" Jennifer's voice quivered. "It's just Uncle Gabe. In different clothing."

Slowly her ragged breaths returned to normal. Her heartbeat slowed as hysteria faded. Megan finally gathered her courage and stared straight into the monster's red eyes.

Deep inside the swirling crimson was a shadow of soulful chocolate brown.

"Gabriel," she whispered.

Gabriel shifted back to his human form. In jeans and a white shirt, he shuffled his bare feet. He looked broken. Megan was stricken by the deadness in his eyes. They were still and dark as a decaying swamp.

He spread out his hands. "I warned you, Megan. This is what I am. You wanted all of me, and this is it."

You promised you could handle what I am. I should have known you'd react just like she did.

Too late, she realized what she'd done. Gabriel stepped back, his expression shuttered. The damage had been done.

He turned to his brothers. "Alexandre, take your daughters to our parents. It's safer there. Rafe take Megan there. I'm entrusting her care to you, my brothers."

"My daughters?" Alex looked bewildered.

"Where are you going?" she cried out to Gabriel.

He spoke tiredly over his shoulder. "I need to be alone for a while."

"Gabriel, wait."

But he did not appear, or choose to hear her entreaty.

Chapter 20

He'd finally opened up and she'd reacted to his transformation as if Gabriel were a demon. Megan stared helplessly as he turned a corner and vanished.

Alexandre looked at the twins in blank confusion.

Swallowing hard, she told him the news. His mouth dropped open. "My babies? Simone's babies? You're alive."

Joy sparkled in his blue eyes. The air of toughness dropped, replaced by tenderness. He stepped forward to embrace them, but the girls shrank back, looking to Megan.

"Megan, is this really our daddy? Will he be like the Normals and hate us?" Jillian whispered.

Their uncertainty tore at her. She hunkered down to their height and held their hands. "Listen to me, sweethearts. We're the Musketeers and we don't lie to each other. Alexandre is your dad and I can sense the love and the joy he feels at knowing you're here. He'll do everything to make you happy. Go with him. He's just like his brother Gabriel, and there's not a mean bone in his body."

Jillian's brow wrinkled. "But you were afraid of Gabriel. I saw in my mind how mean you think he is."

Swallowing hard, she forced a brave smile. "I was wrong, honey. Adults can be wrong, and I certainly was."

Alexandre looked at the twins with such emotion that her own eyes welled up with tears. Jillian and Jennifer approached him cautiously.

"Megan says you're good, and you'll love us," Jennifer, ever the leader, told him.

"Always," he whispered. "Now that you're here, I'm never letting go."

They rushed into his arms and he held them tight. Together they walked to the street.

She turned to face his waiting brothers.

"I'm going to find Gabriel." Arms akimbo, she regarded them with a level look.

"Gabe asked us to watch over you and bring you back to our parents." Raphael folded his arms over his chest. "We're not leaving without you."

"Then stay. I don't give a damn. I can look after myself, but he needs me."

Etienne glared at her. "I'd say he needed you when he shifted. He doesn't need you now. He needs to be alone. I know, I'm his brother."

"And I'm his mate." She softened her voice. "I have to go to him."

Raphael gestured to the shorter, muscular brother. "Dai, take her."

Expecting to be wrenched forcibly away, she faded into Shadow. Damian sighed. "C'mon, Megan. Stop that. I'll take you to him."

"When Draicon fly," she shot back, sidestepping so he couldn't track her voice.

He arched a dark brow and a smile broke out on his handsome face. "I can, and so can my mate, so that qualifies."

"Megan, Damian can teleport you to where Gabe probably is. Where he always hangs out when he needs to be alone. Go with him." Raphael spoke with authority, but his tone was kind.

Using her powers, she cloaked them and when they materialized, Damian had set them by the cover of hedges in a park beside the water. He nodded toward a white statue.

"You'll find him by the statue of the immigrant. He likes to hang there."

Damian released her, his green gaze piercing and intelligent. "Good luck, little Megan. Be patient with Gabriel. He needs you, even if he won't admit it."

He vanished.

Standing by the fence bordering the Moon Walk, Gabriel braced his hands on the railing. He stared at the wide expense of river. Wind brushed back the dark silky hair from his forehead. His wide shoulders hunched.

Suddenly he straightened. He'd caught her scent. She hurried toward him.

"What are you doing here, Megan?"

She gave him an imploring look. "I had to find you, Gabriel. I'm sorry, I'm so sorry, I didn't mean it. It was, just, you looked…I was terrified."

A muscle ticked violently in his jaw. He did not look at her.

"Do I like it? No, of course not. Is it part of me? Yes. Can I prevent it?" White showed on his knuckles as he gripped the railing. His eyes were cold and desolate.

"I've tried. This shift was my first since we lost Amelia and Simone. Seeing that bastard hurt you and the girls brought it out in me."

"And I made it worse with what I said. I can't take it back, Gabriel. I wish I could, but all I can do is keep telling you how sorry I am."

He said nothing. Emotionally, he was as distant as ever. Getting him back would be the hardest challenge of her life. Megan blinked back the burning in her eyes. She had to try.

A low growl rumbled in her stomach. The chaotic fight at the cemetery had lowered her energy levels.

"You hungry?"

Always the concerned Gabriel, thoughtful about her welfare. When she nodded, he sighed. "Let's go to my place. I'll fix you something."

They walked past Jackson Square down a narrow street lined with charming building facades. Gabriel stopped before a brick building with lacework iron balconies. He led her upstairs.

The door he unlocked opened to a small apartment. Worn hardwood floors covered by faded rugs, striped wallpaper and antique, comfortable furniture made up a living area the size of a postage stamp. A video game console sat on the cluttered coffee table beside a stack of books and a violin case. The walls were covered with a multitude of sequined and feathered Mardi Gras masks. Megan touched one particularly beautiful mask. It glittered and sparkled with…

"Are those real diamonds?"

Gabriel nodded.

"Where did you get all these?"

He scrubbed his bristled jaw. "Ah, they're all gifts." His voice dropped. "From former lovers. The diamond one is from a Countess who visited the city for Mardi Gras. She died long ago."

She cleared her throat. "How many lovers have you had, Gabriel?"

Silence for a moment. "Too many. Since Tamara, I've never had a relationship that lasted longer than three nights." His full mouth quirked in a bitter smile. "Longer than the length of the full moon."

Then he looked away again, refusing to meet her gaze.

In the center of one wall was a skeletal mask. Megan shuddered. The mask screamed in abject horror. "This couldn't be a gift."

"No. I bought it for myself when I wiped out Tamara's memories." He turned away, jammed his hands into his jeans pockets. "To remind me…"

He scrubbed his jaw again. "I'll make dinner. My neighbor Stephan should have a stocked fridge. Be right back."

Her stomach twisted in knots. She went into the kitchen, studying the copper pots and pans dangling from pot hooks in the ceiling. The buffed oak cabinets and granite countertops were sparkling clean.

When he returned carrying two large plastic bags she asked, "Is this where you like to hang out all the time?"

He shook his head as he dumped the bags on the counter. "Not always. I stay here when I get in…certain moods. The activity of the Quarter, the tourists and locals, it keeps me…"

Human.

The last word thought, not spoken.

A set of faded French doors led out to a balcony overlooking the street. A small wrought-iron table and chairs along with a futon sofa were on the balcony. Hanging ferns and a faded Mardi Gras gold-and-green mask hung from the latticework. On the railing was a set of black-and-gold beads.

"Make yourself at home. I'll fix dinner."

She sank into the comfortable couch. Lazy chatter from tourists on the street below blended with bleeping car horns, mules clopping by as they pulled carriages and the noisy cheeps of sparrows flying in and out of the neighboring eaves.

Delicious smells drifted through the opened door. Gabriel brought out two bottles of beer, handed her one. He didn't sit close as he'd done in the past, but settled on the sofa's other end.

I deserve that, Megan thought miserably.

An odd-looking decoration of turquoise beads set in string with feathers hung from the ornate ironwork. She asked about it.

"It's a dream catcher. Damian brought it for me from New Mexico, where he rules his pack. Supposed to catch bad dreams and keep them at bay."

"Does it work?"

His eyes, normally a sparkling chocolate brown, were dark and unmoving as swamp water. "No. I had nightmares about you reacting the way you did, and they came true."

Ouch.

Megan curled her feet beneath her. "How far is the famous Bourbon Street?"

Beer bottle in hand, he waved up the street.

She struggled to make easy conversation, but Gabriel remained reticent. Finally, he went inside.

They ate in the cramped kitchen at a small table. He set before her a plate piled high with tasty-looking dishes. Gabriel explained they were red beans and rice and jambalaya with sausage, peppers and shrimp.

He gestured to a plate with slices of crusty

French bread. "Eat those between each course to cleanse your palate and prepare it for the unique taste of the next dish."

After dinner, she helped him clean up and then joined him on the balcony. Shadows lengthened on the streets as dusk fell. Gabriel opened two more bottles of beer for them. They sat on the couch, watching the world below.

"Your accent, it's different from your brothers and the others I've heard here."

Gabriel shrugged. "I moved around a lot, spent a lot of time in southern Louisiana."

A flash of insight. "You're like a Shadow. Only you hide in the open, so others can't see what you are."

He gave a small nod.

The creak of a French door opening drew her attention to the adjacent balcony. A tall, chestnut-haired man wearing low-slung jeans stepped out. Megan's nostrils flared as she caught the scent. He saw Gabriel.

"Hey, Gabe. Haven't seen you around."

"Stephan. How they biting lately?"

The vampire laughed, yawned and scratched

his bare chest. "Not bad." He eyed Megan as Gabriel introduced her.

"You found your mate. Congrats, man."

"Thanks." Gabriel shifted on the couch. "Tell me what's been going on in my city."

Stephen frowned and braced his hands on the railing separating their balconies. "Normal, for the Quarter, except the last couple of days. Very quiet. Too quiet, and some bad mojo in the air. Rumors of demons in town."

Gabriel stiffened. "What kind?"

"Hitchhiker demons, the kind that blend into the populace. Nearly impossible to scent and harder to flush out. Very nasty SOBs. Sorry, Megan. Not even the wolves can detect them. The older vamps have taken to staying close to home. No one wants to mess with these demons."

She sensed Gabriel's disquiet. The same kind of demon had possessed Jay.

Stephan plopped down on a lounge chair, picked up a banjo. He shot Gabriel an inquiring look. "Care to jam, wolf?"

"Why not, vamp?"

The mournful music from Gabriel's fiddle

was soulful and deep, compared to the lively strumming of the vampire's banjo. Megan listened, enchanted as Gabriel closed his eyes and ran the bow over taut strings. His long, dark lashes swept down to his cheeks. He looked absorbed in the music, his expression tender as when he'd loved her.

Would he ever love her that way again? Grief punctured her insides.

A crowd gathered below, and when they'd finished playing, applauded loudly. Stephan gave Gabriel a respectful nod. "Good times, wolf."

"Back at yah, vamp."

Stephan vanished inside, and when he emerged, wore a blue silk shirt, polished shoes and gray pleated trousers. "See yah, pups. I'm going out for a bite to eat."

"Be careful," Gabriel warned.

With a nod, the vampire leaped over the balcony to the street below. Megan watched him peddle away on a bicycle. Little silver bells tinkled as he sped off.

"A vampire on a bike with bells. I'm surprised he doesn't have cards in the spokes," she jested.

Gabriel set down his fiddle with a solemn

look. "The bells are said to keep demons away. Demons like to hop onto motorcycles and bikes, and their spirits get trapped in the bells."

His dark gaze was so intense, she shuddered. "That demon, how did you know Jay was possessed?"

He shook his head. "I honestly don't know. It felt like instinct."

Megan went to take his hand. "Instinct is a good thing, Gabriel. It keeps us alive."

But he sidled away, avoiding her touch. "Instinct turns us into raging beasts. You saw the evidence."

"How long has he lived here?"

"A few years. He does repairs and keeps an eye on my apartment when I'm gone. In return, I give him reduced rent."

At her inquiring look, he added, "I own the building."

"I see. And you rent out to vampires?"

"Vampires, Draicon, even a Fae. Stephan was tossed out of his clan two decades ago for some minor infraction. Sienna, the Fae who has the apartment in the back courtyard, is a runaway. I gave her a job and a place to stay. Sienna keeps the green plants and the gardens in the court-yard."

"Everyone in this building is a paranormal you took in because you felt kinship to them, isn't that right, Gabriel?"

"Yeah. We're all misfits. But I'm the only real monster."

Megan cringed as her own words were thrown back at her. "I'm sorry, Gabriel. I wish I could take it back. I'd do anything to take it back."

A sparrow landed on the railing, cheeped. Gabriel went inside, returned with a plate filled with crumbs. Soon several sparrows began feeding.

"You call yourself a monster and you feed sparrows. Monsters don't play the fiddle or have friendly conversations with their vampire neighbors, either."

"Whenever I shift into a Trans-Feral, it always drains me and I strive to find my human side. It's why I came back here." He leaned forward, resting his elbows on his knees. "My family, I always avoid them afterward. I can't stand the way they look at me after I turn Trans-Feral."

The way you looked at me.

Megan swallowed past a thick lump in her throat. "Fine. We can live here, then. I'll find a job at one of those little shops. I don't have sales experience, but I'm a hard worker and…"

Realizing he wasn't responding, she fell silent. Megan traced a single bead of condensation on her beer as it slid downward. She had no idea how to get him back. Or if she ever could.

A group of people below waved. Maybe she could jerk him out of his inertia. Setting down her bottle, Megan stood up. After grabbing the beads on the balcony, she swung them around her head.

"What are you doing?" Suspicion threaded through his deep drawl.

"Throwing down beads. It's tradition, right?"

The group hooted, hands stretched out for the treat. Megan ran them teasingly between her breasts. She stripped off the conservative white blouse. Below it she wore only the lacy white bra he'd enjoyed unhooking in the dressing room.

"What the hell are you doing?" he demanded.

She aimed him an innocent look. "Isn't this what you do when you throw beads?"

As her fingers reached behind her bra, a deep growl came from his chest. Gabriel bolted off the couch, spilling his beer. He threw the beads down and lifted her into his arms.

"No one sees you naked but me."

"Where are you taking me?"

"Into my bed."

Hoots and hollers of approval sounded below. Gabriel shut the door with a powerful kick and laid her on the bed. Skin stretched tightly over the bone structure of his face, he looked wild and Feral.

"Is this what you want, Megan? Have a wild beast ravage you? Because that's all I am, a monster."

Without fear and in total trust, she looked up into his swirling amber eyes. "You're no monster, Gabriel Robichaux. You promised you would never hurt me and I trust you."

With a wary look, he watched as she undressed. Savage hunger flared in his gaze as she lay naked on the bed.

Her heart pounded in fear, not of him, but of their bond. She'd badly damaged his faith and trust in her. Could he accept her again?

A vein throbbed in his temple as he removed his clothing and joined her. He looked wild, sexy. Amber fully took over his eyes.

Splaying his fingers across the back of her head, he took her mouth. Hard, demanding. When they pulled apart, she put a finger to her kiss-swollen mouth. Blond curls tousled, she felt wild and primitive.

Gabriel put a possessive hand on her breast, flicking the taut nipple. A lick of tension, the air shimmered with danger. Acid sexual need. A cry for something more, deeper.

This was the first step, she promised herself. Sitting up, she slid her arms about his chest.

"I can take whatever you want to give me," she told him.

Intent glittered in his Feral gaze. "Be careful what you ask for, *chère,*" he said softly. "Because I will give it."

"A threat?" Megan traced his lips.

He took her fingers, lightly bit one. "A promise. And when you come, you'll come hard, my name on your lips. Nothing but the feel of me inside you, my body knowing yours, the pleasure I alone can give you."

Sultry and sexy, his mate slid her arms around his neck. Muscles went taut as she kissed and licked his collarbone.

Trust shone in her blue eyes. Not fear.

Passion pushed him over the edge. All he could scent was her musky arousal. His body tightened as she took hold of his stone-hard erection.

Her inexperienced hand stroked him with some hesitancy, then emboldened, she explored. Megan ran her fingers around the head, touching the moisture weeping from his cock. When she brought her wet finger to her mouth, he lost it. Gabriel dove for her.

She rolled away. Playful. Teasing. Want arced the air between them. Megan leaped off the bed, wriggled her hips at him. He gave a low growl.

"A chase? Very well, *ma petite.*"

It didn't last long. He caught her around the bed's opposite side, threw her down. So hard he hurt, he trapped her with his body. Gabriel gazed down at her face.

It was soft with emotion.

Something in his chest batted aside the Feral

beast. Wonder. Deep affection. Despite the hurtful words she'd hurled at him, he ached at the thought of losing her.

He was falling in love.

The thought choked him.

Risk his heart? Not again. Never. Gabriel barricaded his thoughts. Instead, he let the hunger consume him.

The space between her legs grew moist for him. Raw heat fired by the intensity of his need kicked up further. Sensitized, Megan quivered for his touch as he reached for her.

A slow, taunting smile. A lick of his skilled tongue across one breast. A promise of fire.

His teeth on her skin, lightly. Her fingernails on his chest, hard.

He was pure power, his belly flat with defined muscle as she palmed his torso.

"My wolf," she whispered.

An answering growl. Her nipples painfully erect, she pressed against him. He bent and took her breast into his mouth. Erotic heat shot through her, each flame sizzling higher. He released her breast, kissed his way down her body. Fingers tunneled through her damp curls, he sought her heat.

And turned it higher. He teased. Tormented. Pushed her until she shattered with a single cry of his name. Just as he'd promised.

Then he slid between her legs and inside her body in a powerful thrust. They strained against each other. Gabriel growled.

She moaned.

It was raw and wild and earthy. Her own wolf howled in response as climax danced out of reach.

Then he angled his thrusts and the heat burst into an inferno. Megan screamed his name again, as he shuddered against her.

Filling her with his seed, his passion.

His potent Feral magick.

Chapter 21

The sex had been wonderful, rough and passionate, Megan thought.

But they hadn't made love. It was only sex, like he'd had with dozens of anonymous women. Gabriel's mask was permanently back in place.

Deeply troubled, Megan dozed off. A shrill ring woke her up. Gabriel rolled over, snagged the phone.

"Yeah?" His voice was deep, sleepy and sexy. He sat up, scrubbed the dark bristles on his angular jaw. "Ah, damn, forgot. Okay, we'll be there."

When he hung up, he sat on the bed's edge, his long legs dangling off the side. "That was

Raphael. My family is throwing a party tonight at the Blazin Cajun to celebrate the anniversary of the first restaurant opening. Rafe is bringing over your suitcase with all your clothes. We have to be there in an hour. I'll take a shower first."

The bathroom door slammed behind him. Megan put on her clothing, dread pooling in her stomach. Time to meet the parents. Would they accept her?

Or look with silent condemnation in their eyes as his brothers had?

When the doorbell rang, she answered it. Dressed in black leather, Raphael walked inside with her backpack and a plastic garment bag. He set both items down carefully.

"My mate, Em, saw the dress and figured you'd want to wear it tonight, so she had it pressed." He shoved his hands into his pockets and studied her.

Raphael, the Immortal. Megan swallowed past her anxiety and lifted her chin. She stuck out a palm. "We haven't been properly introduced. I'm Megan, Gabriel's mate. It's a pleasure to meet you."

He took her palm and turned it over, staring at the crescent birthmark. Raphael released her hand, his expression shuttered. "Pleased to meet you, Megan. A word of warning. I'd cover up that mark if I were you and curb your powers."

"I'm used to it."

Raphael nodded. "Good. Keep it covered at all times. Even tomorrow at the family picnic."

Her mouth trembled. "Among your family?"

The even look he gave her filled her with dismay. "My parents don't like Shadows."

The Shadow mark burned as if lit by fire. Heat warmed her cheeks. More discrimination, even among his own family?

The Kallan's look softened. "Don't worry, Megan. Gabriel will take good care of you. You'll be good for him."

But as he left, she said softly, "I thought so, too, but now I wonder."

Crowds packed Gabriel's Blazin Cajun restaurant. The turquoise dress made her feel pretty and feminine. Megan touched the covered birthmark, wishing she didn't have to disguise herself.

Gabriel had introduced her around with possessive pride, making her hopeful the rift between them could mend. His parents, Remy and Celine, were so charming and friendly, she wondered how they could have treated Gabriel like a misfit.

Absently she rubbed at her right hand, feeling it itch. Remy came over with a smile, handing her another beer.

"It's crazy, my son's business, everyone wants to congratulate him. He's done good." Warmth filled his gaze. "I'm so glad he found you, Megan. Gabriel has needed a mate for a long time now. You will keep him steady."

She liked his father and made easy talk with him as Remy chatted about the restaurant and his family. His pride in Gabriel was obvious. Yet she wondered how he would have reacted at the cemetery, seeing Gabriel's Feral side emerge.

Megan scratched her hand again. Remy's gaze fell downward.

His smile vanished as he saw the exposed silver crescent moon. Gabriel's father set down his beer. "Please tell me that's a bad joke of a tattoo."

Something inside her snapped. "It's not."

Spotting his wife, Remy nodded. "Come with me, Megan."

She didn't want to, but his firm grip on her elbow left her no choice. Gabriel's father escorted her to a small, private office. Papers were stacked neatly on a crowded desktop beside a sophisticated computer system. She breathed in the reassuring stamp of Gabriel's scent. Celine joined them and closed the door.

"This office is soundproof. We can talk freely," Remy said.

He picked up Megan's right hand and showed it to Celine, who gasped with dismay.

"Another Shadow." The disgust was evident in Remy's face and tone. "You must leave, now, before anyone sees you and thinks we're harboring a fugitive."

Gone was the friendly Draicon who had greeted her with warmth. Megan lifted her chin. "It's okay."

She explained about Tristan giving her full

immunity, along with the twins. Celine and Remy exchanged worried glances.

"Those little girls, Alex's miracles? They are Shadow, as well?" Celine looked upset.

Remy slid an arm around his mate's slender waist. "Don't fret, *chère*. We'll teach them just as we did Amelia. No one will know they're different."

Because different is bad, Megan realized, seeing his expression.

Celine's full mouth twitched. "You must understand, Megan, you can't be seen here. It will hurt Gabriel's business he's worked so hard to build up. It's best if you avoid public contact, as well. We can't risk anyone seeing what you are, immunity or not. Shadows are not like us."

Her mouth dropped. "Are you saying..."

"It's best if you leave now. Tomorrow, at our house, it will be safe to show this." Celine looked upset. "I'm sorry, *chère,* but it's too dangerous to be a Shadow here."

She understood, and yet felt the familiar resentment. Was this what Simone had faced, living with Alex? Always hiding, always told never to fully be herself? It didn't matter if she'd gotten rid of the hated purple tunic that marked her as an outcast. Or if she hid her birthmark.

They'd treat her just the same.

Remy escorted her out of the office. Megan plastered a wide smile on her face to hide her anger.

And the shame she could not avoid.

She found Gabriel sitting at a table, surrounded by admirers. He looked relaxed and happy. Telling him what had transpired would upset him. This was his night. Megan beckoned him and he left his seat.

"I'm leaving," she told Gabriel.

He searched her face. "You're upset. What happened?"

Megan steeled herself and hated the lie forming on her lips. "I'm tired, that's all. It's been a very draining day."

Gabriel glanced around. "I'll take you home."

But someone called his name and he hedged. Megan saw people clamoring for his attention and knew how important this night was to him. It was his "normal" half, the human contact he needed. "Let one of your brothers take me home. It's okay, Gabriel. Stay. You need this."

Worry flashed in his eyes. "I don't like the idea…"

"I insist."

He bent down and kissed her cheek. "I'll be home shortly."

But as Damian walked her to the door and the crowd pressed around Gabriel once more, she suspected he would not be home soon.

Because here, in his restaurant, he could act as normal as his family pleased.

She wanted to scream her outrage for both of them.

Megan paced the balcony. A chill skated down her spine, despite the tide of warm, humid air drifting from the street below. Nearly 2:00 a.m. and he wasn't home yet.

Then she heard a familiar, deep voice singing a Cajun tune. Megan saw Gabriel coming down the street.

His arm was around the waist of a young, pretty blonde wearing a very short pink dress.

The blonde was giggling and curled tight next to him.

A greeting died in her throat. She heard the downstairs door slam. Minutes later, the door to his apartment opened. She sensed him at the doorway of the balcony.

"Why aren't you in bed, asleep?"

"I couldn't sleep, not without you. I was worried about you. Guess that was stupid of me, seeing you have company to keep you occupied."

He came outside. "That was Sienna. She's the Fae who lives downstairs."

"I see."

"Megan, I was taking Sienna home because it was too dangerous for her to walk alone. There are demons out." His voice was gentle.

Jealousy bit her like stinging gnats. "And you had to personally escort her home?"

"She's my employee and a little drunk."

"Fae get drunk? On what, nectar?"

"Champagne. She's allergic. My bad. I thought I'd hidden it away, but she found it. Sienna loves the stuff."

His sudden grin melted her. Megan rubbed

her tired eyes and gave him an apologetic look. "I didn't mean to sound shrewish. It's just that you and me, I want things like they were before what happened in the cemetery...."

How could she explain to him that she only wanted to mend the break between them? Gabriel's grin faded. "It's late and you need sleep."

Suddenly her nostrils flared. "Do you smell that?"

Gabriel went preternaturally still. "Demon." He bolted for the railing, inhaled the air. "It's gone."

"I don't understand. I never was able to scent them before. I've smelled that on the island. That was a demon?"

"Just like the one that possessed Jay." Gabriel shoved a hand through his hair. "Let's get inside."

But in bed, he fell immediately asleep after giving her a small peck on the cheek goodnight. Megan curled into a ball on her side in misery, wondering if she could ever make up for the cruel words said to him.

Or if he'd ever forgive her.

* * *

Gabriel's reticence continued through the morning. Conversation was stilted over chicory coffee and beignets. Only after she dressed in freshly pressed trousers and a dark red crewnecked shirt for his parent's barbecue did he look directly at her.

"You look so lovely," he said in a husky voice. "But you always do."

Breath caught in her throat as he pulled on fingerless leather gloves. In a tight black T-shirt, faded jeans and a black leather jacket, he looked sexy as hell. And dangerous. Gabriel pushed a hand through his long, dark hair and slid on sunglasses. He handed her a helmet.

"Let's go. We're taking my bike."

In the courtyard, the woman Gabriel walked home last night leaned against the brick archway. Yellowed light reflected off the silver glitter in her now auburn hair. She wore a baggy blue T-shirt and sleep shorts. A silver and copper bracelet with a snake's head adorned her left wrist.

Her face was a delicate blue, contrasting with her large gray eyes. Megan tried not to stare.

The woman hiccupped. She gave Megan an apologetic smile. "Hi, Megan. I'm Sienna. Thank you for letting Gabe escort me home last night. I was scared to walk alone, and I was drunk. I must look pretty green to you."

"Not really." Amused, Megan bit back a smile.

She touched her face. "Oh, no. Am I blue? I must have really overdone it."

"A little."

"Sorry. I must look an awful sight."

Gabriel hooked his thumbs through his belt. "I told you to lay off the champagne. Your hair is red again, too."

"Oh dear." Sienna turned to Megan. "Gabriel's wonderful. He's like my big brother, took me in when I couldn't even find a safe street corner. Usually I'm not this bad. It's all this weirdness in town. I got scared."

Sympathy filled her. She liked Sienna and sensed a kinship with her, another creature in need of refuge. "Why are you scared?"

"I ran away from an arranged marriage and there's a hefty reward for finding me and bringing me back. I'm good at masking myself, but…" Sienna hiccupped. "When I drink too much, I'm toast."

Gabriel sighed. "Stay inside the next few nights and have someone else cover your shift."

The Fae looked upset. "I have to earn my keep."

"Earn it next week when you can better disguise yourself." He gave her a stern look. "That's an order."

Sienna put a hand to her head. "I'm not arguing with you. My head hurts too much." She gave Megan a pretty smile. "I'm so glad we met, Megan. You'll be good for Gabriel. I've been worried about him, he's been alone too long."

The Fae waved as they left.

They rode on his Harley out of the French Quarter. Her thighs spooned against his muscular ones, Megan hooked her arms around Gabriel's waist. A warm wind whipped at her shirt, blew at her face. Wanting to laugh for the sheer joy of feeling free, she snuggled closer against his broad back.

A flash of his thoughts tore through her. The

yo-yo of longing for her and need to protect his heart. Because she'd broken it quite effectively.

Throat tight with emotion, Megan loosened her grip.

At his parent's house, the Cajun barbecue was in full swing. Delicious smells of spices and food threaded through the sound of loud laughter and conversation.

She was meeting Gabriel's family. His pack. Anxiety ratcheted up a notch.

Gabriel and Megan walked around to the backyard. Conversation died as everyone turned to regard them.

Judging from the stony faces, she knew Remy and Celine had told everyone she was a Shadow. Megan steeled her shoulders and felt a warm arm slide around her waist.

Gabriel gave her a friendly wink. *It's okay,* chère. *They're just a little surprised. They'll warm up to you.*

The chill dissipated slightly as she greeted his brothers. Gabriel introduced her to Indigo, a tall, muscular man with tanned skin, and his lovely vampire mate, Avril. Jamie, Damian's mate, was friendly as she jogged a small, adorable baby in her arms. The mates of Gabriel's other brothers greeted her kindly.

But Remy and Celine acted polite and distant. Though Celine served all the other guests the hot food, she discreetly ignored Megan.

I will never be welcome here, Megan realized as Gabriel fetched her a plate piled high with steamed crayfish.

As he talked with his brothers, she spotted the twins sitting on a picnic bench. Megan set down her plate and a smile died on her face.

Gone was the laughter and the shining joy. Jennifer and Jillian were two solemn toy soldiers, dressed alike in blue short sets. Their spines ramrod straight, they did not speak.

Megan squatted before them. "Hey, sweeties."

They greeted her politely. Her heart sank. "Why aren't you playing?"

Jennifer's lower lip trembled as she squeezed Jillian's hand. "Gramma and Paw Paw told us we can't play unless we're being supervised. No more hide-and-seek. They said we shouldn't ever use our magick. They said Shadows aren't normal."

Patting their hands, she went to find her mate.

"Gabriel." Megan plucked at his leather sleeve, urging him to follow her. At a discreet vantage point, she gestured to the girls. "I know things aren't right between us, but this is important. Look at the girls. They're afraid to move out of fear of displeasing your parents."

His eyes narrowed. "What about my parents?"

"They told them that Shadows aren't normal." She plucked at the pretty dress. "The girls escaped discrimination on the island only to be treated just the same here. It will never change."

He took a long, hard look at her, then the twins. Gabriel's mouth tightened. He set down his beer and took her hand.

"C'mon."

When they reached his brothers, he dropped her hand and gave Alexandre a long, level look. "Alex, *mon frère.* Do me a favor. Take the twins and get them far away from here."

Etienne choked on a sip of beer. "Say what?"

Gabriel ignored him, folding his arms across his broad chest. "Don't let them feel like they can never measure up just because they're Shadow. Promise me that, Alex. I can't bear for them to be treated like I was. Or make the same mistakes I made and cost more lives like Simone and Amelia."

Alex's blue eyes narrowed. "Gabe, what the hell you talking about?"

Gabriel gestured to the silent twins. "Look at them. They were overjoyed to be with you last night. Kids having fun. Now our parents are turning them into shadows of themselves. Ironic, huh? They don't like Shadows and Jilly and Jenny will pay the price."

Alex studied the girls. "Damn. It's happening all over again."

"I already caused you to lose Simone and Amelia. Don't lose them, too."

The twins' father said something that sounded like a Cajun curse. "I've told you again and again, Gabe, it wasn't your fault."

"It was. You had something good and honest and pure, and I took it all away from you. Because I was arrogant. I could have hidden Deke away in another safe house. But I didn't. I brought him here, to our house."

His voice dropped to the whisper of dead water. "I wanted all of you to see me as heroic because I personally saved a Shadow. I thought it might wipe out your fear of my Feral side. And Simone and Amelia paid the price."

Raphael looked stunned. Grief twisted Alexandre's face while Etienne and Damian stared.

"You never told us, Gabe. I never imagined you felt like this. Why didn't you tell us?" Raphael rubbed the back of his neck. "*Merde,* why have you kept this from us all this time?"

"You didn't kill them," Alexandre said quietly. "Logan's son did."

Gabriel looked impassive. He pushed back at a fallen lock of his hair. "I was responsible."

"I couldn't tell, man, you never let on how you felt. Why didn't you tell us?" Raphael seemed like a scratched CD, repeating the same line over and over.

He said nothing. Then Alexandre nodded slowly. "Because you never let on about anything, do you? All you ever do is smile or echo our emotions when something bad happens, when it's acceptable to be sad or angry because we feel the same. You've always hidden yourself away. Like the day you were left behind. You waved goodbye as if nothing were wrong."

Raphael stared at Gabriel. Grief etched his

younger brother's expression. "I looked up to you, man, I idolized you. You were the one who kept me together, the one who was always calm and collected. And now I'm finding out I never knew you all along?"

"Guess not. Things can get a little hairy with me."

"Stop it," Raphael burst out. "Just stop it, Gabe, goddammit! Always with the damn jokes, the act!"

"Would you rather see me turn Feral? Megan has. I'd say she'd rather have the jocularity."

She couldn't let this drag on a minute more. "No, I wouldn't. I'd rather see you as you are, Gabriel. Angry. Sad. Happy. I care only about you."

Gabriel gave her a wary look, but she took his face between her palms.

"All of you. Not just the part you show to the world. I'll never let go, no matter what. Understand? I don't care what your brothers think, what your family thinks. I care about you, whoever, whatever you are. I'm with you all the way."

He gave her a solemn look. "All the way,

Megan? Enough to bond fully with me and exchange powers? Would you see yourself become a Trans-Feral, because that's what will happen."

A small fear flowered as she recalled the glowing red eyes, the blood dripping from his talons. "I'm not going to lie, Gabriel. I am afraid, but I'm more afraid of losing you."

Gabriel gave a small, but very honest smile. Hope filled her. Maybe they could start over.

"I'll take the girls away tomorrow," Alex decided. "Thanks, Gabe. I guess I was too blind before to see it, and too blind now."

Her mate mock-punched his brother in the arm. "Are you too blind for a quick game of football?"

Raphael's face cracked into a reluctant smile. "You two are slower than a tortoise. Easy game."

"And you're too busy tripping over your own feet," Etienne mocked.

Megan laughed, glad the camaraderie had been restored. She headed to her abandoned plate of crayfish as the game began.

Her mate raced backward to toss the ball. She

sat on a chair, hungrily tracking him as smooth muscles flexed. The tight jeans hugged his taut ass. Gabriel caught her staring and winked.

Blushing, she sat back.

They could make it. She felt certain of it.

And then all her hopes were crushed like seashells beneath a steamroller.

Chapter 22

In the midst of the game, Tristan materialized. He caught the ball and squeezed. It deflated instantly.

Her heart pounded hard as the Immortal paced toward her. Gabriel wiped his brow and raced to her side as his family drifted over, looking bewildered. He snapped an order for the women to hustle the children into the house. Looking scared and uncertain, Jenny and Jillian went with the others.

"What the hell are you doing here, Phoenix? No one invited you," Gabriel demanded.

"I'm here for Megan."

Pulse racing, she shrank back as Gabriel snarled. "You promised not to turn her or the twins over."

Tristan laid a hand on Gabriel's wide shoulder. "I made the promise not to turn Megan or twins over to Enforcers. I never promised I would not take Megan back to Shadow Island."

The Phoenix studied her with his piercing cold eyes. "If you come with me, Megan, the girls may remain with their father."

"That's what you wanted all along, isn't it? You want to bring me back to Shadow Island, to face punishment and banishment." She stepped back, her heart racing in panic.

They would beat her, then dump her in isolation. She would never be among another living being again, but spend her days alone. It was the worst torture for a Shadow.

"No." Gabriel stepped forward, pushed Tristan out of the way. "Take me."

His gaze never left Megan. "Leave her alone, and make your promise to include giving Megan her freedom forever, and the twins to remain with Alex. Honor the pledge I made to you, Phoenix. Fair trade."

Tristan seemed oblivious to the loud protests, and Gabriel's brothers, who looked like they would strangle the Phoenix. "It is a fair trade," he said slowly. "I will honor it."

"Gabriel, what promise? The one you made to him back at the house?" Megan asked.

He took hold of her trembling, clammy palms. "The promise I made when I was ten, Megan. Tristan wanted to lock me up for good. He released me on one condition. He said when the time came for him to take someone I cared about, he would let them go if I finally went to prison. A fair exchange."

"You can't do this." She turned to Tristan. "Lock him inside a demon prison until he dies!"

"He's a dangerous Trans-Feral and the prison at Donaldson is the only facility that can effectively contain savages like him." The Phoenix's face was harsh, his tone impartial.

"He's no more savage than you and I," she insisted. "No one taught him to curb his powers when he was growing up. Everyone was too afraid of him."

"Are you not afraid of him, Megan? A Trans-Feral who would tear you to pieces?"

"He'd never hurt me. He's been nothing but

gentle to me and the twins. He's only a danger to his enemies."

"And yet you called him a monster." The Phoenix's tone was gentle.

Ashamed, she looked away.

Tristan snapped heavy silver handcuffs on Gabriel. Her mate flinched as the metal touched his wrists. She felt his pain and knew these were no ordinary handcuffs, but burned his skin and kept his magick suppressed.

"No," she whispered. "Don't do this to him."

The Phoenix ignored her. She turned to Gabriel's parents, who stood by in mute shock. "You can't let him do this. Do you know what they'll do to him in there? They'll torture him, he'll die! Please, help me! Stop this."

But they remained immobilized. Tears blurred her vision. Her entire body shaking, Megan flung her arms around Gabriel. "You're not taking him," she screamed at Tristan. "I won't let you."

"Megan." Gabriel's voice was soft. "C'mere, *chère.*"

Broken, she faced him. He lifted his cuffed hands and cupped her face, gently wiping away her tears with his thumbs. "Look at me, Megan. It'll be okay. This was meant to happen a long time ago. It was inevitable."

"I won't let you go," she choked out.

"You must." He kissed her mouth and whispered into it. "Go with Rafe and Em. They'll keep you safe. That's all I care about now, you and the twins, and Alex will never let anything happen to them. I want you to live."

Not without you. Never without you. "I love you, Gabriel, I've always loved you, but I was too stubborn to tell you. Please, don't leave me."

Tristan pulled him away. "Time to go."

"No," she screamed.

Gabriel glanced at the Kallan. "Take care of her, Rafe. I'm entrusting her to you." He gave her a tender look. "Love you," he whispered.

Then Tristan waved his hand and they vanished.

She screamed, falling to the ground. Her chest hurt, her stomach did a sickening spin. Megan wept, and then scrubbed at her face, letting the anger take over.

Standing, she glared at his parents and lifted an accusing finger. "This is my fault, but it's your fault, too. All he ever wanted was to be normal and accepted. And you were too afraid of him, couldn't work past your fear, to make him feel that way. You drove him into prison. All of you. I hope you rot in hell for what you've done to my Gabriel."

Remy looked stricken as Celine began to sob uncontrollably. As Remy led his mate into the house, Raphael rubbed the back of his neck. "Megan, come inside."

She told him to do something nasty in Cajun French. His eyes widened. She braced herself for the retribution. Instead, he sighed.

"We'll work this out…"

"No, we won't. I'm going after him." She dusted the fertile Louisiana soil off her shaking hands. "Where is this prison in Donaldson? Take me there."

Raphael gave her a level look. "No."

"Fine. I'm going myself. I'll find it." She had no money, no resources, but hadn't she escaped from Shadow Island? "Just stay out of my way."

"I can't take you there." Raphael heaved a deep breath. "I promised Gabe I'd keep you safe."

"But I didn't," Etienne ventured. "I can take you there, but it won't do any good. We have to try something."

"We can break him out," Damian offered.

Raphael shook his head. "I've been there. No way can an ordinary Draicon get out of there. You'll die trying. I'm Immortal, let me do it."

"And you have a pregnant mate you need to protect." Etienne shook his head. "I'm the eldest. I'll do it."

"We will," Damian and Indigo chimed in.

"I owe him one for my beautiful girls." Alexandre's eyes narrowed. "Rafe, you said no Draicon can break out. But Gabriel isn't an ordinary Draicon."

Raphael's dark eyes widened. "Damn, you're right. But even one Trans-Feral can't take on the Crimson demons guarding the prison."

"What about two?"

The men turned to look at her.

"Two Trans-Ferals would give him a fighting chance," Raphael said slowly.

Indigo shook his head. "If only there was another Trans-Feral in existence."

Megan's heart raced. "Not yet. But there will be after I get into his cage."

Damian frowned. "How can you…" His green eyes widened. "The mating lock."

Sweat beaded her brow as she clenched her hands. "It's the only way."

She was still partly afraid of what Gabriel was. But every cell cried out for her mate.

Megan looked at Etienne. "Take me to him."

His brother glanced at the sky. "Tomorrow. It's not safe now. Tomorrow, when the sun is high, I'll do it."

Clad only in a pair of cut-off jeans, Gabriel sat inside the silver cage. His arms wrapped around himself, he constantly shivered.

Every time a demon neared, his Feral side took over. The constant ping-ponging of the transition was taking its toll.

Seeing a demon walk toward the cage with his dinner, Gabriel fled for the sheltered part of his cage. The "house" was private, surprisingly comfortable and spacious with room enough for him to stand upright, as if to encourage him to remain in human form. It had a wide bed, a small kitchenette with table and chairs, night-stand with a good reading lamp, a separate bathroom and shower. Even some of his pre-cious books had been transported here.

Luxury for a prison.

Then again, considering how long he'd be here…

Suddenly a delicate scent of flowers filled his senses. Weary, he lifted his head and inhaled. Gabriel peeked outside the shelter, suppressing his Feral half by sheer will.

No one was in sight as the demon shoved in a bowl of bloody entrails inside his cage, then closed and locked the door.

The fragrance lingered. Drew closer.

Naked, Gabriel sat on the bed, his heart beat-ing furiously. Daring to hope, afraid to think the impossible.

Megan materialized before him. She wore the turquoise floral dress he'd bought her.

Fearing he had hallucinated, he closed his eyes until two warm, soft hands cupped his face.

"You're not dreaming. I'm here, Gabriel." She kissed him.

Oh, it was the softest satin, this kiss. Megan's scent flooded his nostrils. Gabriel remained still, drinking in her mouth, not wanting the dream to end.

Then she took his lower lip between her teeth and bit lightly. Mischief glowed in her beautiful blue eyes as he regarded her.

"Megan?" He wrapped his fingers around her slim wrists. His heart burst with joy, then reality set in. Gabriel looked around grimly.

"You have to get out before they discover you're here and lock you up for good."

"I'm not leaving." She turned up her face to him. "Call it my right to a conjugal visit. I want to make love with you, Gabriel. Achieve a mating lock and become what you are."

"No. I can't allow it. You have to leave."

"Breaking in is easier than breaking out. If I have your powers, we can both break free. Make me Trans-Feral, Gabriel. It's the only way you can protect me in here."

Hissing, he pushed a hand through his rumpled hair. "I can't make you what I am."

"I want you to."

Sincerity shone in her shining blue eyes. "And

when I do, I'm shifting into a Trans-Feral and we're breaking out of here."

"You would do this for me? A monster?" He traced the fragile bones of her face with a wondering finger.

"Not a monster. My mate, who is loyal and brave and sacrificed himself for me." She took his fingers, kissed them one by one. "Can you ever forgive me for saying those terrible things to you?"

"I already have," he said solemnly. "I need to know, Megan. Why did you react that way when I'd already warned you?"

As she confessed about her nightmare, he listened. Gabriel slid a palm over her nape and caressed her scarred skin. "I wish I could have taken those dreams from you. Why didn't you tell me before?"

"I was afraid it would make the dream more real." Megan leaned against him. "Now my worst nightmare is never seeing you again, never being with you. Not having your acceptance."

"You have more than that. You have my heart."

It was comforting and yet terrifying seeing

her trapped here with him. The cage was a haven and a curse. "It's like us," he realized slowly. "We've both struggled for years to be free and not have our own people fear us, but now we can't hide from what we truly are."

"But together we can stand strong. Then nothing will knock us down."

He took her hands and kissed them. Gabriel gave her a wry look. "I'm dressed for the occasion, but I need a shower. C'mon."

Megan shivered as he gently undressed her. The bathroom in his cage was surprisingly large. A shower in one corner took up half the room. He stepped into the glass enclosure, herding her before him.

Jets of warm water cascaded over them. Gabriel lifted his face to the refreshing spray. Muscles rippled fluidly beneath his sun-darkened skin. Water beaded in the dark hairs of his chest.

Megan began to soap his sweating body, running the cake over his thick muscles. He tilted back his head and released a contented sigh.

"No one ever cared for me the way you do, *chère,*" he murmured.

She delighted in scrubbing the muscle and sinew, making him shudder in pleasure. When he turned to face her, his thick arousal slid against her belly. Megan encircled it and stroked with her wet hand.

His eyes snapped open. Amber flared in them. Gabriel took the soap and began washing her.

With slow circular strokes he washed her breasts, teasing her nipples until she arched and moaned. Then his wet, soapy fingers slid between her legs.

Megan whimpered as he caressed and played with her. Hot whispers in her ear, a promise of sultry heat. Gabriel watched her. Possessive pride filled his dark gaze. Then he ceased and cupped her bottom with his strong hands, pinning her against the ceramic tiles.

Gabriel nudged her legs open with a knee. With one smooth move, he slid into her body. She gasped as he stroked, his thrusts steady as the water beat down on them.

One hand continued to hold her upright. With his other, he cupped the back of her head and took her mouth in a savage, deep kiss. She arched against him, crying out.

"Come for me, darling," he whispered.

Megan screamed into his mouth, squeezed his arousal, feeling him pump deep inside her. Shaken, her body well used, she opened her eyes. Lungs squeezed air in and out as he dropped his head. Gabriel pressed a singularly sweet kiss to the juncture of her shoulder and neck.

"I'll never leave you, Gabriel."

"You're not afraid?" Challenge filled his gaze.

"Not as long as you're with me."

"Then, come here."

The bed dipped beneath their weight as they fell naked upon it.

His hungry growl echoed her own. Megan arched her back, leaning into his caress as his hands touched and explored. Wonder dawned on her face.

Love filled him. For her. His Megan.

Without words, he pushed into her. Breath fled her as his thickness filled her to the core. He thrust, withdrew and created a rhythm, intensifying the pleasure. Their fingers intertwined as he smiled tenderly at her.

Craving her, needing her, as equally as she needed him.

Megan arched as she opened to him like a flower. Then she felt him tense as his hands gripped her hips. His cock seemed to expand and stretch her beyond limits.

Framing his face, she let him feel the gentleness of her love for him. Gabriel took it, absorbed it, cherished each mote of sensual tenderness.

Megan wrapped her legs around his pumping hips as he angled his thrusts to give her the most pleasure. She arched off the mattress as the tension built. She felt taut as a bowstring, her wolf howling.

"Megan, come for me, now," he commanded.

Sweet tension shattered. He loved the pleasure hazing her face, felt pride in her climax as she sobbed and clung to him.

Gabriel groaned, his big body shuddering as he joined her. He opened himself as he filled her with his seed. The sensual haze blended with the powerful emotions flowing from him. And then he felt it.

He locked inside her as his essence flowed into her. Megan gasped in wonder. "It's happening."

Colors swirled and sparkled, dancing in the air like fireflies. He felt his spirit pour into his mate. His powers. His fears. His love.

She opened herself fully, giving him all her Shadow powers. Her tearful gaze locked with his intent one. For the first time, Gabriel felt completely one with her as they exchanged powers. He felt her every emotion like a brush of silk across his quivering body.

They were sealed together in the flesh and the spirit.

Chapter 23

Megan lay drowsily splayed over her mate's body the following day. A heart that belonged solely to her beat reassuringly beneath her cheek. She felt sated, her body tender and well-loved.

She pushed a lock of silky hair away from his face. "I smell demon."

A lazy stroke over her naked thigh. "We are in a demon prison, *chère.*"

"No, this smells different. Bitter, more pungent." Megan frowned. "It's gone now, as if someone covered it up."

Hearing voices outside, Gabriel frowned. His nostrils flared. "Get dressed. My family's outside."

Near their cage, his brothers and their mates

and his parents stood with J.P. Sacks, the governor of Shadow Island and all the members of the Draicon Council, including the leader, Morgan Bailey. Suspicion pricked him. Something felt very off and it wasn't because of the unusual assembly.

Megan slid her palm trustingly into his. He gave her a reassuring smile and narrowed his gaze at his father.

"What's going on? Here to stare at the animals?"

Remy looked guilty. "Your brothers and their mates, they convinced me…"

Jamie stepped forward. Determination hardened her pixie face. "I told Remy that Megan shouldn't be ostracized because she's a Shadow and this business of keeping you locked up because you're Feral, Gabriel, well, it's…"

Damian cursed in French.

At her mate's words, Jamie nodded. "Exactly. What our son does in his diaper. Look at me, my magick is powerful. I'm capable of flight. I know other Draicon are sometimes afraid of me, but do they stick me on an island because I'm different?"

Damian snarled. "I'd kill them if they tried. Just as I'll kill anyone who tries to send you back, Megan."

"But to keep it civilized, to show we're not beasts, we put on a little pressure." Etienne gave the council a hard look.

"We're springing you, too, *mon frère*," Raphael told him.

"And no one's ever locking you up again," Alexandre said.

"Or we'll deal with them," added Indigo, flexing his strong arms.

Remy gestured to the council. "We all had a long talk. Then I called in a large political favor with the council and requested a meeting with them and the governor. They held a vote and agreed to free you and Megan, under conditions."

"I was outvoted." Bailey gave him a sullen glare. "You belong in prison and Megan Moraine is too dangerous to be released to the public. She's a Shadow."

A sibilant hiss sounded as Governor Sacks pointed at Megan. "She goes with us. I will not honor that vote, Robichaux. That abomination belongs on my island."

Pulling his mate closer, Gabriel growled softly. "Where you can abuse her and send her to a sex shop like you have other female Shadows? She's mine, Sacks. Back off or I'll rip you to pieces, cage or no cage."

"Stop it." Remy turned to the governor. "You made a deal and you're not breaking it. Or I'll have my sons demonstrate how the Robichaux pack deals with those who betray me."

The pale-haired governor warily watched as the brothers shifted into wolves and snarled. They could make short work of the whiny bastard.

Though he was heartened to see family support at last for Megan, it troubled him that no one stood up for the other Shadows.

As his brothers shifted back, Remy approached the cage. "Son, the council's agreed to free you and Megan under my strict supervision."

"What's the catch?" Megan asked.

Remy hedged. "Before you leave, both of you must be fitted with a restraining device to suppress all your magick powers. I know it sounds bad, but you will be out of this horrid place."

"I will not leave this cage until all Shadows are free." Gabriel leaned against the bars, dimly wondering why the magically charged silver didn't diminish his powers.

"Gabriel." Rapt wonder shone on Megan's face. "Why would you would do this for my people?"

"Because until they are all free, you won't be. You're wholly part of me now, Megan, and what affects you is important to me."

"You make no sense, Gabriel," Remy cried out. "You and Megan can both walk out of here."

"I have to make a stand, *mon père,* for what I believe in." He drew in a deep breath. "Because I know how it feels to live as an ostracized Shadow. All these years I've tried to act like nothing mattered, hide myself so no one could see inside me. You said I would always have trouble blending into the human world. You feared my Feral side."

He glanced at Megan. Her deep blue eyes were soft with emotion. He drew strength from this.

"What matters most to me now is that she's with me. She loves me, despite of what I am. Megan sees past the mask that hid me from the outside world, into the heart of me, and she still loves me. She's chosen not to abandon me. I would die for her before because instinct drove me to protect her beyond all reason."

Emotion clogged his throat. Gabriel locked his gaze to Megan's, seeing the tears fill her eyes. "I would die for her now simply because I love her. So I suppose I am more human than you ever thought."

He felt only her love, her devotion. Gabriel slid both hands into hers.

"He's right. If you release us," Megan told them, "then release all my people."

"When hell freezes over."

This from Sacks. Bailey nodded. "You're staying locked up."

Then Gabriel caught a whiff of something foul. He inhaled, gagging on the pungent stench of sulfur and methane.

Demon.

But no Crimson demons were in sight. And

this odor, he'd smelled it before, back at the cemetery when Jay had been possessed....

Shock stilled his heart. He narrowed his eyes and forced himself to truly see those standing before him.

Fury consumed his body. He telegraphed to Megan a silent order just as Sacks inched backward and grabbed Celine. A sickly smile touched the governor's thin mouth. "Fine. But I'm taking someone with me to Shadow Island to face punishment."

All hell broke loose as his family rushed toward the governor, only to be blocked by a powerful force field thrown up as Bailey held out his hands.

Gabriel saw red. He roared and shifted into Feral.

The bars bent easily beneath the power of his hands. Dimly he realized Tristan had not caged him in a special prison meant for Trans-Ferals.

He leaped out of the cage. Megan pushed past him.

Talons grew out of the governor's fingertips. He sank them into Celine's chest. "I'll rip her heart out," Sacks snarled.

Gabriel's blood pressure dropped as his mother screamed in terror. He tested the force field and broke through, and then ground to a halt in shocked wonder.

Megan transformed into a Trans-Feral. Her red eyes glowed with purpose, not savagery. She broke through the force field, grabbed Sacks and tossed him. The governor flew through the air, crashing against the cage. On him in seconds, she raised her right hand to swipe at him with her talons.

Sacks snarled and lashed out at her.

Only to find Megan had vanished. Sacks screamed. Blood gushed from a terrible wound on his chest. Blow after blow rained on the governor.

Gabriel went for Bailey. The council leader's eyes glowed red as he attacked. Using his powers, Gabriel tore the man to pieces.

It was over. The dead bodies of Shadow Island's governor and the head of the Draicon council lay on the ground. Bits of splintered bone and blood scattered over a wide path.

Gabriel shifted back to human form and went to Megan. Her body was shaking badly, her red eyes filled with blood tears. *I can't do it. I can't shift back.*

"It's okay," he soothed. "Just think of things that make you human."

Finally, she assumed her human form. Naked, she flushed with embarrassment. Gabriel waved his hand and clothed her, erasing the blood splatters from her body. He slid his arms around his mate.

"I saw what you were, and for the first time in my life, I felt only a sense of pride and wonder in my abilities. Not shame and disgust," he told her.

His family looked stunned. Celine put a palm over her bleeding chest, whispering thanks to them both.

The four remaining members of the council were pale with shock. "What, what was *that?*"

Tristan materialized out of thin air. "*That* being how the head of your council and the governor of Shadow Island were actually hitch-hiker demons, or *that* being what Gabriel and Megan did?"

Gabriel hugged Megan, wondering what

awaited them. If need be, he'd fight tooth and nail to keep her safe. She smiled at him.

You don't have to, my love. I can fight tooth and nail and fangs now.

Joyous laughter spilled out of him. No matter what, he knew he finally had someone at his side who understood and accepted him.

Tristan's gaze softened. "I had to lock you up, Gabriel, to see if Megan would do what destiny called for her to do. To finally lose her inner fear of what you are and bond with you in the flesh and the spirit and the heart through the mating lock."

"To become Trans-Feral?" Megan asked.

"To exchange your powers." Tristan poked at the governor's remains with the toe of one biker boot. "Trans-Ferals have been extinct so long, Draicon forget their true purpose. Trans-Ferals are the only Draicon who can scent, flush out and kill any kind of demon. Demon magick doesn't affect you. Ten years ago, a few hitch-hiker demons escaped their prison in the other dimension. When they possess a body, they blend perfectly. Even when they become cruel, no one questions them because they have positions of power. After time, the host ceases to exist, his soul trapped forever with the demon's until his body dies."

"You put me in a demon prison to make me constantly shift." Gabriel realized the clever ploy.

Tristan nodded. "You'd denied yourself so long, you needed to exercise the power to gain full strength."

His piercing green gaze filled with intelligence. "Two invisible slayers to kick demon ass will be a tremendous asset to hunting down the escaped hitchhiker demons."

"Does this mean we're free?" Megan asked.

The Phoenix's face cracked into a wide smile. "Both of you." Then he sobered. "Pay attention to your dreams, Megan. They aren't nightmares, but visions to prepare you for the future. Share them with Gabriel."

Her eyes widened. "The creature in my dreams, it was Gabriel."

"The creature wasn't going to hurt you, but your own fears made him into something he wasn't. You have the gift of prophecy. No one ever taught you how to examine your visions and separate your emotions from the truth—" he glanced at Gabriel "—just as no one taught Gabriel when he was much younger how to harness and control his powers."

Tristan studied the council. "I suspect there's a meeting I'll be sitting in on, where I'll act as the fifth member when the council votes to lift the suspension on Shadow Island. Gentlemen?"

Not giving the shaken council members time to react, the Phoenix waved his hand. He vanished along with the council. Gabriel hugged Megan to his side.

No longer ashamed, he felt a quiet sense of pride as he saw newfound respect on his family's faces.

"I was afraid of you ever fathering children, Gabriel. I hoped the recessive gene would die with you. I'm ashamed to say I thought you were our family's biggest liability. You're not. You're our biggest asset." Remy's voice dropped to a grieved whisper. "I'm so proud of you, my son. I wish I had told you that before. That I hadn't treated Simone and Amelia like I had."

Gabriel walked over and hugged his father. "It's okay, Papa. Everything will be fine now."

"Will you and Megan come live with us?" Celine removed her hand from her chest, which had started to heal. "We would be honored. Until we build you a house of your own, Gabriel. For when the babies come."

Knowing her dream, he glanced at Megan's shining eyes. "If Megan agrees. That place of mine in the Quarter is more suited to a bachelor."

"Yes," she said, nodding her head. "Yes, yes and yes!"

His parents smiled.

"I suppose this means I truly do belong somewhere now." She reached up for his kiss.

"Always," he said solemnly, as he bent down to take her mouth. "Right here at my side."

Epilogue

"I'm full. Please. No more. Thank you for coming over and bringing coffee and dessert."

She pushed back the china plate of homemade blueberry pie. "See? I ate everything, Celine."

"But, *chère,* you must keep up your strength." Kind brown eyes, as dark as Gabriel's softened. "And what is this *Celine?* I asked you to call me Maman."

She dabbed at her eyes as Celine rubbed her back.

"It's normal, Megan. Every woman gets emotional afterward."

A chorus of voices agreed with her. She smiled at her sisters-in-law.

"We'll come over any time you need good, old-fashioned womanly support. Because the men sometimes, well, they just look too confused to figure it out. Even men who have extraordinary powers," said Emily, who was rocking her baby, Sam.

Once she thought no Draicon could ever be called friend. Now she had a supportive family of Draicon.

She wasn't alone anymore. And never would be, not with Gabriel's strong, powerful family as her allies. All Shadows had been freed and the Draicon who'd used the females as sex slaves sent to prison. Shocked and humiliated at knowing they'd been controlled by a powerful demon, the council had lifted any restrictions on Shadows. Tristan promised to find the missing Shadows and offer them a normal life among a Draicon pack.

Gabriel had gone on a little hunt of his own and now Devin, the man who'd nearly assaulted her on the boat, was locked in a demon prison.

Excusing herself, Megan walked to the large, comfortable bedroom she shared with Gabriel. The door was slightly ajar. She pushed it open and lingered in the doorway.

In the rocking chair Remy had bought for her,

Gabriel sat holding their six-week-old daughter. With some awkwardness, but growing experience, he cradled the newborn. In his deep, soothing tenor, he crooned tenderly to their baby.

Emotion filled his dark eyes as he glanced up at her. "She's sleeping."

Megan went to him, caressed his cheek. "Because she loves her daddy's voice, and only he can make her sleep."

He brushed his lips against the thick down on their child's head, then picked up her tiny right hand to display the silver crescent moon birthmark. "But Amelia is her mother's daughter."

They didn't know yet if their baby would be Trans-Feral. But with each passing day since the birth, Megan felt Gabriel's fears ease. His family would help train Amelia and teach her to control her enormous powers.

"And then there's also Amelia's godfather, who just happens to be a very powerful Immortal." Gabriel grinned, reading her mind. "Tristan would never let anything happen to her."

Megan pulled up a chair to sit beside him.

"She's safe, Gabriel. It's a new world she's been born into. A good one."

"Unreal," he murmured. "I can't believe you and I did this. The Shadow and the Trans-Feral."

"Learned to change a diaper?" she teased.

Gabriel's expression filled with love as he gazed at her. "Created a miracle."

* * * * *